J. H. Magee

Night of Affliction and Morning of Recovery

An Autobiography

J. H. Magee

Night of Affliction and Morning of Recovery
An Autobiography

ISBN/EAN: 9783337099558

Printed in Europe, USA, Canada, Australia, Japan

Cover: Foto ©Raphael Reischuk / pixelio.de

More available books at **www.hansebooks.com**

THE

NIGHT OF AFFLICTION

AND

MORNING OF RECOVERY.

AN AUTOBIOGRAPHY.

BY REV. J. H. MAGEE,

PASTOR OF THE UNION BAPTIST CHURCH.

CINCINNATI, O.
PUBLISHED BY THE AUTHOR, 12 RITTENHOUSE STREET.

1873.

INTRODUCTION.

DEAR READER:—Permit me to introduce you to a sketch of the author's life during twelve weary years of suffering, which he is pleased to call his NIGHT OF AFFLICTION AND MORNING OF RECOVERY."

Though the night of my suffering and pain was long and cheerless, yet, as the darkest night has its morning, so my afflictions terminated in an entire restoration to health. The darkest cloud has a silver lining. "And it shall come to pass, when I bring a cloud over the earth, that the bow shall be seen in every cloud." The bow of God's promise was seen on the dark clouds of the night of my affliction as a token of God's goodness to me. It was through my afflictions that the word of truth was made a blessing to my soul.

For some time before I obeyed the call of God to begin the work of preaching the glorious gospel of Christ, I felt an overpowering love for the Bible, the word of God. In 1858 I went to the village near which my father's family resided, and bought a reference Bible—the first book of the kind I ever bought with my own money. From this precious treasure I learned to love God and his word and work more and more. I have this Bible now, and would take no money for it. "Buy the truth and sell it not." Prov. xxiii. 23.

After I entered the ministry I felt the necessity of a thorough training in theology, as well as that amount of mental training which is calculated to fit a minister for a sphere of extended usefulness. The signal manner in which God answered my request in this case will be seen by the following extract which I wrote about two years before the request was actually granted: "I have felt the importance of some training in theology, and shall never be satisfied until I have obtained that amount of theological training which is necessary to the successful preaching of the gospel. It has been my desire for some time to have an opportunity of studying at the Pastors' College, London, England. Whether this shall be attained or not remains with the great God who holds the destinies of men. I shall trust Him for guidance, believing 'that all things work together for good to them that love God, to them who are the called according to his purpose.'"

God began to answer this prayer by placing me in the way of Elders Caldicott and Carto, of Toronto, Canada, from whom I received much instruction. From the latter I purchased five volumes of Dwight's System of Theology and five volumes of Doddridge's Works, which laid the foundation for a systematic course of study.

About two years after I wrote the above extract, I was permitted to cross the Atlantic Ocean, and to enter Mr. Spurgeon's college, in which I had my long-cherished hopes and wishes fully satisfied, viz: of learning how to preach in such a manner as to win souls to Christ. "O magnify the Lord with me and let us exalt his name together. I sought the Lord and He heard me, and delivered me from all my fears." "This poor man cried and the Lord heard him, and saved him out of all his troubles." Ps. xxxiv. 3, 4, 6.

Now, dear friends, the main objects for which I have written this book are the following: To encourage the faith of believers in the Lord Jesus; to believe what He says:—"Hitherto ye have asked nothing in my name; ask and ye shall receive, that your joy may be full." And again He says: "Ask, and it shall be given you; seek, and ye shall find; knock, and it shall be opened unto you; for every one that asketh receiveth, and he that seeketh findeth, and to him that knocketh it shall be opened." Therefore, my friends, if you want to know the fulness of joy you must love God, ask in prayer for what you want in the name of Jesus, and expect and wait for an answer.

The book is also designed to afford comfort to all who are afflicted, or who have known some of the sorrows of life, and it is hoped it will supply a long-felt want among our colored people for works from the pen of one of their own race. The author claims for it a simple narration of facts which came under his notice during his night of affliction and morning of recovery, and hopes and prays that the volume may prove a blessing to all its readers, especially to such as may be in the night of affliction, and that such may realize, by an humble trust in Jesus, that the night of suffering shall be exchanged for a morning without clouds. "And he shall be as the light of the morning when the sun riseth; even a morning without clouds, as the tender grass springing out of the earth, by clear shining after rain."

If this volume shall bring comfort and peace, through the blood of Jesus, to one poor sorrowing son or daughter of suffering humanity, I shall have been sufficiently rewarded for the time and labor spent in writing it.

Remember that all things work together for good to them that love God, and that we have the precious promise of an abiding and present Christ always, even unto the end.

That the Lord may bless this work to the lasting good of all who may read it is the prayer of

Yours, truly,

J. II. MAGEE.

Cincinnati, O., June 2, 1873.

CONTENTS.

CHAPTER I.

CHILDHOOD AND YOUTH.

CHAPTER II.

THE COMING AFFLICTION.

CHAPTER III.

AFFLICTION'S DREARY HOUR.

CHAPTER IV.

THE DAWN OF HOPE.

CHAPTER V.

ON THE ROAD OF PROGRESS.

CHAPTER VI.

AN AWFUL TRIAL.

CHAPTER VII.

THE MORNING COMETH.

CHAPTER VIII.

CANADIAN PROSPECTS.

CHAPTER IX.

LIFE IN TORONTO.

CHAPTER X.

THE OLD WORLD.

CHAPTER XI.

LONDON, THE METROPOLIS OF THE WORLD.

CHAPTER XII.

THE HAND OF THE LORD.

THE NIGHT OF AFFLICTION, ETC.

CHAPTER I.

Birth—Parentage—Removal from Kentucky—The rented Farm —The fallen Cupboard — The Locust Trees — Removal to Macoupin — Prairie Scenes — My first School — My Color a Source of Discontent--Reflections.

I was born in Madison county, Illinois, June 23d, 1839. My parents were born in Kentucky. My father was what is called "free born," but my mother was not so fortunate. She was born a slave, belonging to Billy Smith, of Louisville. My mother, being a slave, naturally prevented her uniting with my father in marriage until he had paid what her owners were pleased to term her equivalent in money. The sum was set; he began to make strenuous efforts to raise the required amount. He had a great reputation as a pork packer, in which capacity he worked several seasons I have heard him say that he has worked all day, stopping just time enough to take his supper, and then set in again for the night, working till day-light in the morning; and so on for weeks. Finally the sum for which he so ardently sought was raised, and paid over to Mr Smith, after which they were united in marriage.

Having spoken so much in reference to the manner in which my father labored to secure the freedom of my mother, and thus become her husband and protector, instead of leaving her in the bitterness of slavery, I must not fail to speak of the noble manner in which my mother labored in assisting to repay my father; which she has done a hundred times over. They removed from Louisville to Madison county, Illinois. Mother, with her own hands, has wrought many a live long day, both in the house and in the fields. On one occasion she took her little boy, Lazarus, to the field, there being no one to leave him with at home. She placed him near an oak tree, which had been dead, seemingly for years, thoughtless of any danger befalling her child. She went to work; two or more hours elapsed, during which time, at intervals, she went to see how the little one was getting on, then to her work again. In a little while she noticed that the wind had begun to blow quite briskly; at length she heard from the direction she had left little Lazarus a great noise, as of the falling of a tree; she looked—and, oh horror! the tree beside which she had left little Lazarus was blown down. In haste she ran, and found the brains of her darling boy oozing out of his ears—life was extinct, one of the limbs of the tree having struck him on the head. All who have the least feeling of sympathy can readily judge of the pangs of poignant grief with which her heart was pierced. All this intense grief was brought about by the monster Slavery, it being the primary cause. Will not the Lord avenge his own? Have not the tears of my mother, with those of thousands of mothers, gone up to the throne of the Eternal? Will He not regard them? Does not the blood of my brother, with that of thousands of my fellow-countrymen, cry out from the ground? Surely the eye of Omniscience has not been closed to all this.

The old rented farm on which my parents first settled is frought with the recollection of many happy scenes of my childhood. The bright, long, summer days, which I thought were much longer than the days of summer are now,—it was then that my heart was first impressed with the beauty of the exterior world. The first song of the robin, announcing the happy return of spring, awakened notes of gratitude to God. The fall of the year was always a season of much pleasure to me, it being the time when the farm products were taken to Alton, the nearest market. This afforded me a favorable opportunity to go to "town."

My parents brought a large cupboard with them from Kentucky, with a large number of plates and cups and saucers, which belonged to my grandmother—such as would now be termed "old fashion tableware." This ware afforded the first means of awakening a desire in my mind to learn to read from studying the different designs with which the ware was marked. One day my sister Elizabeth removed the cupboard and the ware to the yard, to wash and re-arrange them. All the ware having been washed and placed in the cupboard by my sister—to see how it would look—when a brisk wind came and blew the cupboard and its contents to the ground, smashing all the ware into atoms. Thus passed away one of my childhood's first teachers.

In front of the old homestead of Mr. Dorsey stood a number of tall locust trees. Beneath these trees was spread, on a temporary table erected for the occasion, the wedding dinner of my brother, Samuel Magee, who married Miss Catherine Stewart, at the age of nineteen. This was the first wedding dinner I ever saw. I have often spoken of the wedding dinner which was eaten beneath the locust trees in front of the house.

Several years having elapsed after the marriage of my brother, when he took a prospecting journey to Macoupin

county, in search of a site for a farm. He was successful
in purchasing a site for a farm containing one hundred
acres, twenty of it being in timber. William, Alfred, and
Samuel Magee went immediately to breaking the prairie,
preparatory to removing to it. A house was soon erected
for the convenience of "the prairie breakers." The family
growing anxious to get to their prairie home, could not
wait until the farm was made ready for their reception, so
an adjoining farm was rented to which we were removed
early in the spring, and made preparations to put in the
spring crop. I think we remained on that farm two years,
We then removed to our own prairie home. Prosperity
shone upon our pathway for several years, God blessing
the labors of the family most abundantly, so that whatever
they laid their hands to prospered.

The scenes on the wide prairies of Illinois are at times
fearfully grand, especially in autumn, when the Indian
summer sun tinges the horizon with purple and gold.
About that time fires, great prairie fires, were of frequent
occurrence. The grandeur of the scene could be seen for
miles; the angry flames leaping and dashing forward like
the waves of the sea in a terrific storm. As soon as the
fire was discovered, if it was coming towards the farm, it
was necessary to plow several furrows between the fence
and the fire, to keep it from burning up the fences. Wild
deer were frequently seen bounding across the almost
illimitable prairie with a speed at which they only can
travel.

I was sent about this time, for the first time, to a school.
I was delighted at the idea of going to school—the place I
had often heard of but never seen. My father went to the
teacher of the district school, Mrs. Tunsil, who taught in
what was called the Merryweather district. My brother

Alfred and I went to this school for some time—indeed, until the school was closed. Mrs. Daniel Barton was next engaged to take charge of a colored school held in a house on the east side of the farm, which was built for my brother Samuel. The whole family attended this school for several sessions. I was next sent to the Brooklyn district school, to which I went for some considerable time. At length prejudice began to show itself on the part of the parents of some of the children, which was communicated to the trustees. Many of the parents of the children were perfectly willing that I should go to school with their children, but there were others who thought their children were too good to go to the same school with a colored person. The trustees thought it best, for peace sake, to have my parents withdraw me from the school.

Come near all ye that fear the Lord, and help to solve this wonderful problem: because my skin is dark and theirs white, therefore I ought not to have the same privilege of improving the immortal mind. Is this in accordance to the divine will? Is this that charity which alone is the means of knowing our identity as a servant of God —an heir of righteousness? I have not so learned Christ. I think that Christ died for ALL, irrespective of color, and that all the natural blessings with which he has crowned the human family, such as mental and moral training, should be shared by ALL, irrespective of color, creed, or clime.

Notwithstanding all these difficulties, God abundantly blessed me. When one door was closed another was opened. Thus it was at the time referred to. A school was opened immediately after this by a white lady exclusively for the benefit of colored children. I went to this school for six months, after which I was detained at home

2

to attend to duties connected with the farm. During my
absence from school I never forgot the instructions which
I received while at school.

CHAPTER II.

The Coming Affliction—Reflections—The Decrees of God—Stir-
ring Scenes—A Thought yet Future—The Brightening Sky—
My Sister Elizabeth—Her Dying Request—Her Death—My
Coming Affliction—A Soliloquy.

TIME in its onward flight rapidly bore me to the tide
of sorrow and affliction. Like the coming storm, which
gathers in darkness and tempest before it makes its descent to the earth. The morning's sun may have risen
bright, giving its light and heat to thousands who, like the
sun, rejoice their daily duty to fulfill. But ere it has
reached the zenith portentous clouds may have overcast
the sky, spreading darkness and gloom where before was
light and beauty. The hitherto serene sky may be marked
with the dark thunderclouds, upon which the fierce lightning may play in terrific grandeur. The decrees of God
respecting this world may to the unobserving seem but an
idle tale. But does that in the least retard its coming con-
summation? The antideluvians, hearing by the mouth
of the servant of God concerning the coming affliction—
the deluge—thought it a thing quite improbable, judging,
doubtless, from the then clear sky. But how soon, alas!
was their incredulity punished with the terrible vengeance
of God. When, perhaps at midday, the sky gathered
blackness, and the distant thunder became more and more
audible, the forked lightning, as the bolts of Jehovah,

starting athwart the sky,—how changed the scene! The merry dance is ceased; the voluptuous music hushed; the trembling bride and groom amazed; the merchant astounded at his desk, perhaps pen in hand; a moment of dismay. The revellers' feast is as gall in view of the terrible approach of the righteous decrees of God. The coming affliction is at hand.

There is yet another decree to be fulfilled, in the destruction of the present material world, by that most terrible of agents, FIRE. It is in time yet future, and therefore many look at the present and the past, and conclude that surly the great structure of this world cannot be reserved to fire. The faithless and unbelieving will assuredly be visited with the great displeasure of God in the great day of the Lord. That awful day will surely come. The appointed hour makes haste, when the sky shall grow bright with the descending Jesus, with the clouds for his chariot, myriads of angels constituting his retinue, accompanied by the voice of the archangel and with the trump of God. That voice shall doubtless wake the dead with the cry "Come to judgment, come to judgment, come to judgment." The dead in Christ shall rise first. They that are alive and remain shall be caught up together with them in the clouds to meet the Lord in the air. What a scene will then take place! The internal fires, which now hold their seat in mid earth, will then burst forth from thousands of pores, leaping up, up, and up, till the heavens being on fire shall melt with fervent heat. Where are the gosple haters? Where is the blasphemer? the reviler? the drunkard? the sinner of every description? Listen! Hear them calling to the rocks to fall on them, to hide them from the wrath of the Lamb. Methinks the rocks will cry, "Sinner, I'm not a hiding place for thee." This is a description of coming affliction.

My sister Elizabeth for six years had been the wife of Canard Arbuckle, during which time she was almost a constant sufferer both in body and mind. Previous to her marriage she gave her heart to God. She was one of the best christians I ever saw; patient under the most severe trials to which it is the lot of christians to be subject. She was baptized into the fellowship of the Salem Baptist church, Wood river, Madison county, Illinios, and continued a consistent member of that church until God released her from the church militant to go to the church triumphant, in glory. She fell sick in the winter of 1850, and died near the first of March of that year. Before she died she called all the members of the family to her bedside, beginning with father and mother, and admonished each to meet her in heaven. At that time every soul in our family was in the gall of bitterness but my then dear, dying sister. I remember well when my time came to go to the bedside of my sister to hear her dying request; I wept bitterly when she took me by the hand and addressed me—"Henry, I am going to my Father's house in heaven. I want you to be a good boy. Be kind to your mother and father. Meet me in heaven." The Piasa people came a distance of five miles, sometimes every evening, to see her, and hear her talk during her illness. Old christians said that they never had heard anybody talk as she did. Her conversation was all about heaven, and its eternal happiness. Sinners were deeply convicted at hearing a recital of what she had said. When the message came she was ready and willing to go. She asked not to stay, but often said she did not want to stay, that she wanted to be with Jesus. She passed quickly over the river death, shouting ever and anon as she was passing through its chilling waves. She had an abundant admittance into the heavenly kingdom. Farewell, gent'e sister! Thou, who in life was so kind, and in death so solicitous for us. Farewell, till the morning—that bright and hallowed morn of the resurrection—when by the grace of God I shall meet you again. I shall again grasp that hand with which thou didst mine so fondly press. Thou art gone but not forgotten ; thy memory is still dear to many a kindred heart.

Sister, thou wer't mild and lovely,
Gentle as the summer breeze,
Pleasant as the air of evening
When it floats among the trees.

Peaceful be thy silent slumber,
Peaceful in thy grave so low ;
Thou no more will join our number,
Thou no more our songs shalt know.

Dearest sister, thou hast left us,
Here thy loss we deeply feel ;
But 'tis God that hath bereft us--
He can all our sorrows heal.

Yet again we hope to meet thee
When the day of life is fled ;
Then in heaven with joy to greet thee,
Where no farewell tear is shed.

The loss of my sister had scarcely passed before the shadows of the coming evil of my affliction might have been seen looming up in the distance. Already the angel of protection might have spoken to my happy youthful spirit, " Let thy heart cheer thee ; enjoy the few fleeting hours of merry childhood; look upon all, with a heart enraptured with delight, that this beautiful world affords to cheer the spirit of untrammeled, happy childhood; for soon the scene of thy present joy will be turned to one of sore affliction, such as will scatter the present sunshine of thy joy to the four winds."

The bright days of health and happiness soon terminated before the coming affliction, which came like the fury of a tempest, withering the flowers which I had so fondly cherished, leaving nought but sadness, pain, and misery. The quickened step of youth was suddenly stopped. The eye which glistened with health and joy was overcast with the dullness of sore affliction. Like the pride of the forest, suddenly stricken by the fury of the hurrican, causing his leaves to wither and drop in the midst of life. So sudden did my affliction come that none of my people could imagine how or by what means so terrible a disease had come. Little dreaming of the real cause of my distress, that the serpent of a man, whom my parents had nursed in the lap of kindness, had bitten their son almost to the death. May God forgive them for so cruel a deed—a deed the effects of which I fear I shall not soon get well of. May God perfect me through suffering, and at last bring me to the enjoyment of youth and vigor in the fair climes of unclouded day. Amen.

CHAPTER III.

Man that is born of woman is of few days and full of trouble.—Job xiv. 1.

How soon, alas! are the flowers of morning withered; ere we have time to admire the freshness of their bloom they are withered away; a fitting emblem of the days of our probation here. We scarce can possession boast before all that we claim dear, as the apple of the eye, is fled and gone. Look at the beauties of creation as displayed in the vegetable kingdom on a morning in June—how bright and transporting the scene! The birds from almost every tree-top seem to vie with the beauties of the morning. Look again, after a short time has elapsed, and behold the change. The flowers that were once so beautiful in color and fragrant in smell are withered; there is nought but the wreck of departed glory. The birds, which were once the embodiment of happiness, are flown to other and more genial climes. Nought remains but the sad remembrance of departed joys.

Thus it was with me. Twelve years of sad affliction have marked my life with its saddening presence. The early morning of my life was like that of the spring. My prospects bright, life and health as good as the prospects seemed, but it was soon terminated by a fearful disease which blasted all my dearest hopes for the anticipated bright future. As the disease waxed stronger my strength waned, and my hopes of recovery from the malignity of the disease seemed to have vanished like leaves seared by autumnal frosts and blown from their fastenings by the winds of winter. Listen attentively and I will tell you the manner in which I was attacked.

It was near the middle of September, 1853, that I went on a Sunday to a neighboring family who lived one-half mile distant from our house near the thriving village of Shipman, in the county of Macoupin, and State of Illinois. The family whom I have referred to had been for some time considered by us as being our nearest friends, in consequence of which the master of the house made free to ask my father, who was in good circumstances, for small loans of money occasionally. It so happened that the man in question came to my father for the loan of five dollars, which loan he, my father, refused on account of the approaching harvest, which would demand all the money he had in making preparations for it. This refusal so incensed the would-be borrower that he then and there made a dreadful threat: "You shall never gain anything by not lending me that money." A few weeks after the above occurrence brought me to the house of the family mentioned above. The hour for dinner having come, I was invited to dine. The rest of the family drank milk or water, but I was supplied with tea. Strange indeed that they should prepare tea for me who at that time was a mere boy. After dinner I was taken suddenly ill; indeed, so much that they feigned to be greatly alarmed, and hurried me home lest I might become so ill as to be unable to get there. On the way home I got so very sick that I was compelled to stop by the way several times in order to gain sufficient strength to walk home. When I had arrived home it became painfully evident that I had been poisoned. You may shudder at the thought, dear reader, and exclaim, POISONED! Yes, it was really so.

The next day I was removed to what we children called the big house; and there I remained for eighteen months a sufferer from poison which that family gave me in retaliation for my father refusing to lend them five dollars. The suffering I endured those months can never be told; language fails to tell the tale of woe. The winter following the autumn in which I was poisoned my bones began to protrude through the skin so much that my dear mother had to beat the white of an egg into a sort of paste with which she annointed the broken skin. At length it was removed from my body into my limbs and settled there, the effects of which may be seen to this day.

Just above the left knee the limb was swollen so greatly that the skin actually bursted. After this took place I could feel the bone exfoliating. Suppuration immediately ensued, which continued to render me more and more helpless. About the 10th of February, 1854, a worm came from my left knee through an orifice made by the exfoliating bone. This worm was about twelve inches in length, and about the size of a common pipestem. How it got into my limb I am not able to say. I hope some physician, in whose hand this work may fall, will explain it. About the same time that I discovered that the disease had fallen into the left knee, I also discovered that the right foot was seriously affected with the same complaint. At night I could distinctly feel something crawling over my foot similar to those insects which are found under old fallen trees, commonly called, in the west, wood lice, but as soon as a light was procured that painful sensation ceased. In a few weeks the right foot was so badly swollen as to appear like anything else than a foot. Very soon a large tumor appeared on the heel, which in a short time broke and suppurated greatly. As time wore on the heel bone became quite visible, and continued more and more so some months, when, in trying to move it about, I struck it against something, which caused me pain the equal of which I know I shall not feel again, unless it will be when my heartstrings are being severed by death. All of a sudden I reached down and took hold of the bone, and with my own hand I pulled it out. The two little ankle bones on each side were also broken loose and came away, the prints of which may be seen to this day.

Permit me now to call your attention to other scenes of

3

distress which took place among the farm stock, of which
my father had a great variety of what the neighbors said
was of the very best. We will first take a look into the cow
yard, which contained twelve milch cows, which afforded
the chief employment of my mother. Every night either
one or two, and sometimes three, of those cows died, until
there was none left. The next object to which I wish to
call your attention is the pen of fatted hogs, which were for
the winter market and also for our own use. I disremember
the exact number, but to the best of my knowledge there
was about forty head, every one of which died in the same
manner as the cows died. Three of our best horses also
died in the short space of one week; one of which died
under the most wonderful circumstances I suppose the
world ever heard of. It was in this wise: My brother-in-
law, Conard Arbuckle, started on horseback for a doctor
who lived forty miles distant. When he had got about half
way, the horse's belly actually bursted open, and his entrails
spilled out before the animal fell to the ground. He unsad-
dled the animal, put the saddle on his shoulder, and walked
to the nearest settlement of colored people, called the Ridge
Prairie settlement, where he found an old gentleman whose
name was Lee, whom he prevailed upon to come to see me;
for he had not gone to the place where the doctor lived for
whom he had started.

Doctor Lee, being somewhat skilled in the healing art,
came and administered to my sufferings, which somewhat
relieved me, but not enough to enable me to get out of bed.
Doctor Grinstead, a white physician, who lived in a little
place called Woodburn, was next called in. He attended
me faithfully for three or for months without doing me the
least good, first trying one thing and then another. One
time I remember his tying a string to my great toe, and then

fastening the other end of the string to the bedpost. This was done in order to straighten the foot, which had already begun to turn downward. We next called in Dr. John Ash, of Brighton, Macoupin county, Illinois, who attended me faithfully for a great while, during which time it became obvious that I was sinking each day under his treatment. He called a consultation, consisting of himself and Dr. Grinstead, both of whom pronounced me incurable. He therefore told my parents that it was useless to try any more remedies, as he had used all that he knew anything about without even bettering my condition.

For a long time I was without any medical attention whatever; like an abandoned ship without a compass or rudder left to the mercies and uncertainties of the sea. My sufferings continued until somebody told my parents of some doctress living in St. Louis, Mo., whose reputation was great as a cure-all. Father and brother Alfred went to St. Louis, and upon inquiry found the lady in question, who, without being told by my father or brother, told them what they had come for, and that he had a son that was very sick, and how, and for what cause I was sick. This wonderful doctress was employed, and brought immediately to our place, a distance of forty miles from Shipman, the place near which we lived. The doctress having arrived made extensive preparations towards administering some medicines of various mixtures, consisting of poultices, bitters, etc. In a short time I began to mend, and continued to gain strength until I could be lifted from my bed to a chair. This was with great pain; it seemed as if every drop of blood was a nerve, every one of which was being pricked with scores of needles; every joint felt as though it was dislocated; my head like a spinning top. This cannot be wondered at when it is considered that eighteen months had elapsed since I had stood or attempted to stand erect. I could not stop longer than five minutes out of bed, so weak was I from the length of time which had passed since I had been up, and from the loss of blood consequent upon the continual drain from my system made by the protrusion of bones.

About this time I was visited by a man of God, a minister of the Presbyterian denomination. He read from the word of God to me and tried to impress upon me the necessity of seeking an interest in the Savior. Many has been the time that he has stood by my bedside and preached to as many as could gain admittance to the house. During all my dark days of affliction I did not fear death, neither did I think I should die; but entertained a hope of recovery. Often my poor mother has stood by my bedside watching, expecting every breath would be my last. She would sometimes say—" Henry, are you going to die?" I would look strangely and wildly into her face and say—" No, mother, I am not going to die." I recollect of my dear brother-in-law, who is now gone to his rest, standing by my bed one night about ten or eleven o'clock watching me, thinking that every moment would be the signal of my departure, when he thought he heard my teeth clinch. He called the family in astonishment, telling them that he had heard me clinch my teeth, and therefore he thought I was dying. Ah no! it was not time for me to go then, for my heavenly father had chosen me for a work—the work of preaching the unsearchable riches of Christ and his atonement. Often when I think of the goodness of God and the hundreds of deaths through which he has brought me, I am made to weep tears of gratitude for his wonderful mercy in delivering me from the power of death.

The next attempt I made at getting up was more successful. I was taken from my bed and carried by my mother to a chair, where I sat for some time. This was repeated every day until I began to get more strength. Finally I invented a new way of locomotion (for I was still unable to use my feet) by sliding from place to place something like a babe just learning to crawl. The next step towards advancement was walking by means of crutches, which I used for nearly a year. At last I threw away the crutches and walked by the assistance of a cane.

About this time my brother Samuel and his wife came home on a visit from Racine, Wisconsin. Having been sent to the district school until I was rejected, I had received a good start in the acquirement of the rudiments of some of the English branches. Hearing of the great advantages afforded by the schools of Racine to colored youths, I immediately resolved to go; for be it remembered that I had early imbibed an insatiable desire for knowledge, which desire has not yet been fully satisfied.

CHAPTER IV.

THE DAWN OF HOPE.

Introduction--Conviction--A Series of Meetings--Conversion—Doubts--Baptism--Happy in the Lord--A Trip to Racine, Wisconsin--Appearance of the City—Preparation for School—Teachers--Pleasant Associations—Sunday School--Benevolent Society--Home--Chicago--A Loss--Perplexity--Safe at Last--Continued Afflictio--Avenues of Usefulness.

THE darkest night has its morning; the cloudiest sky its sunshine. The night may be dark, and amid its dark shroud may be many an anxious heart anxiously looking for the first streaks of the rosy morning. Ere the songsters begin their matin songs, the bright wings of aurora drives with the speed of thought the retreating night. The mariner looks out first upon the troubled deep and then upon the stormy cloud, upon the face of which the forked lightning is seen amid its terror and grandeur. Then he listens with awe to the deep-toned thunder, which is as the voice of God saying—" I am the God of the mighty deep as well as the God of the heaven of heavens and of the material world." After the storm there is a calm, so deep an one that one might well believe in that power which said to the waves, " Peace, be still."

Thus it was with me. I was a child of affliction, ten pest tossed. I was among the shadows of death's dark night with nought to cheer my lonely and dreary solitude. I had continual sorrow in my heart, which was renewed at opening day and closing night. I looked at the birds, the happy birds of spring, which none can be happier, apparently, than they, and wished from the innermost depth of my heart that I was as happy as they. The glorious sun seemed to shine dimly, and cast a cheerless gloom upon everything upon which it shone. The iron had entered my soul, and I could not be comforted until Jesus came to my relief.

A series of meetings were in progress at this time in Piasa church, five miles distant, to which we were wont to go every evening. The meeting was conducted by the pastor, Elder J. H. Johnson, who was assisted by Elders R. J. Robinson, W. Broner, and H. D. King. My brother, W. H. Magee, was the first to receive conversion. He came home on the night of his conversion and told us of the great things the Lord had done for him, urging my father and mother to go to the meetings, and try to find an interest in the precious Savior, who had been so precious to him. With great reluctance I went to the church and took a seat far back in the part of the church next to the door. The meeting commenced; God's spirit was manifest; sinners went flocking to the anxious seat; but still I sat until the meeting broke up. Oh how terrible was that night to me! It seemed as if everybody was going to heaven but me. I began to reflect. I thought of the trying ordeal through which I had waded. I began to weep, and wept until I could weep no more. Night came again and found me in the house of God. This time I went about half way up to the pulpit. The meeting having begun, sinners were called to seek the Lord while He might be found.

The spirit strove to bring me to bow; sinners were falling on all sides; mourners were rising and telling what a dear Savior they had found. This was too much. I yielded, and was assisted to the mourner's bench, for I could not yet walk without either the assistance of a cane, a crutch, or some person. I prayed that night in all and every way I knew how, without receiving the wanted change. On the next evening I went again to the anxious seat. Towards the close of the meeting for that evening I felt that God for Christ's sake had pardoned all my sins. I went to brother John Samuels that night feeling a great deal better, but not thoroughly satisfied, for doubts had placed me in a very unpleasant condition. I consulted some of the converts as to the cause of my disconsolation. They told me that Satan had caused me to doubt the effectuality of God's grace, hence my spiritual darkness. However, as I grew older I also grew stronger, and was enabled by grace to say to Satan, " Get thee behind me."

On the fourth Sabbath of February I was baptized, in company with a number of my fellow converts. The day was cold but the heart was warm, therefore the cold could do us no harm. I think that was one of my early happiest days, for I have seen many far happier since, and I can say with perfect fidelity, that I enjoy religion a great deal more now than I ever did before in all my life.

For a long time after my conversion I felt that my way to heaven would be one of unclouded joy and peace, such was my peace of mind. For months I never had a cross; indeed, when I listened to those who had a longer experience in the christian race, I would wonder whether it would ever be my lot to pass through such trials and bear such crosses. The word of God shone as a lamp upon my pathway, and I could claim each promise mine. It was a custom of my brother William Magee and myself to engage in secret prayer every morning within our little, humble bedroom, before getting ready for breakfast; and then again my brother, being older than I, took the lead in holding family devotion every morning and evening, each of us, with father and mother, taking turns in leading devotion at the family altar:—

> God of the morning, at thy voice
> The cheerful sun makes haste to rise,
> And like a giant doth rejoice
> To run his journey through the skies.

This was a favorite hymn of my brother William. He is now gone to sing with the angels in that sinless country whose light is the glory of God and of the lamb. My favorite evening hymn was:—

> The day is past and gone,
> The evening shades appear,
> O may we all remember well
> The night of death draws near.

I have thought of the bliss of departing from this life to be with Jesus as calmly as the evening draws the curtains of the night after the sunset of a summer day. O sing to me of heaven when I am dying, that angels may catch the

music of your songs as I pass with them to my bright home
on high.

> Come sing to me of heaven,
>   When I'm about to die;
> Sing songs of holy ecstasy,
>   To waft my soul on high.

> There'll be no sorrow there,
>   There'll be no sorrow there,
> In heaven above, where all is love,
>   There'll be no sorrow there,

> Then to my raptured ear
>   Let one sweet song be given;
> Let music charm me last on earth
>   And greet me first in heaven.

On the 15th of October, my brothers Alfred, Samuel and
his wife, and I started for Racine, Wisconsin. We arrived at Chicago the next morning, after a ride of fourteen
hours. From thence we took passage on one of the Lake
Michigan steamers, which in due time brought us to the
wharf in front of the beautiful city of Racine. I was greatly
impressed with the appearance of the city; its greatest
attraction to me was the number and beauty of its churches.
Give me a city well laid out with God's buildings, and these
well filled with people on the day for divine service. Having rested ourselves and made ourselves as much at home
as it was possible for us to do, we made inquiries respecting
the various schools, about their rules, terms, etc.

Finally my brother Samuel went to see the principal of
the city high school, Hon. W. H. McMynn. Suffice it to
say we were gladly received and treated very kindly by all
the teachers and scholars of all the departments. Having
been examined we were sent to the intermediate department,
in which three hundred scholars were in attendance, all of
whom we found most agreeable; for be it remembered that

my brother and I were the only colored boys in the school. I must now enter into a short description of the honorable teachers of our department. The first whom I shall describe is Professor A. H. Flint, head master of our department, and teacher of mental and moral philosophy and the higher mathematics. He was a most excellent teacher, ruling his pupils with love mingled with rigor. The next teacher to whom I shall introduce you is Miss Ellen Porter, teacher of English and mathematics. This lady was very kind to all her pupils. "None knew her but to love ; none named her but to praise." Her sister Helen often assisted her in teaching; Miss Helen also taught in the third sub-department. While too much can not be said of all the teachers in the way of commendation, yet I will say that Miss Porter has few equals in point of moral and intellectual excellence.

Our progress while at this school was considered better than that of any scholar in school, considering our disadvantages. Having spent considerable time within those halls of learning, we concluded to return home. During our stay in Racine we had formed many pleasant associations, whose memory we shall never forget while the vital fluid continues its course in our veins. I may mention the pleasant association I formed with the Sabbath school held in the First Baptist church, of which Elder Stearn was pastor. I was a regular attendant of the Sabbath school held in that church. The class to which I belonged was taught by Miss Lucinda Morey, a very devout young lady, who had early been brought to Christ, and was a member of the Baptist church. The next social gathering was a society called the Benevolent Society, to which brothers Samuel and Alfred and I belonged; its object was to relieve the distressed. On the 4th of April, we gave a grand supper, in Union Hall, in behalf of the society, to which all the members turned out in their full dress. With banners, upon the folds of which were various devices, floating in the breeze, we marched to the spacious hall. After listening to several speeches by gentlemen who were invited for the occasion, we sat down to a sumptuously prepared supper. Justice having been done to the many good things under which the table fairly groaned, we exchanged many good-nights and dispersed, feeling better and happier for having joined the Benevolent Society of Racine.

Having left school, with all its pleasant associations, we began to make preparations to start home. It was with great difficulty that I could muster courage to leave my teachers, for I respected them very highly. Time with his rapid flight brought us to the day which we had fixed for our departure. It was the 5th of April—I shall never forget it, for it was with great difficulty that the steamer could land. The wind blew fiercely from the north-east, making what the northerners call "a north-easter." A large portion of the pier was washed away, leaving but a single plank for the passengers to walk a distance of twenty feet. I well remember the tremor that seized my frame while I stood first looking at the angry waves which were nearly even with the pier, then at the plank across which I must go, or be left. However I was relieved of my perplexity by a gentleman taking me by the shoulders and hurrying me across. In a short time we were under way for Chicago, arriving there about 2 o'clock that afternoon, where we had to wait for the evening train for Shipman—our destination. While we were waiting for the train at the depot, my brother Alfred, to whom I had given my money for safe keeping, was tacitly relieved of a five dollar note of the money by some of the light fingered gentry of that place. What I should do to get home I did not know, for we had just enough money to take us both home before the other was stolen. All at once a happy thought entered my mind —for Alfred to get his ticket as he was the larger, and I would take what money I had and give it to the conductor, and ask him to let me go home for half-fare. All right so far. We took our seat in the train, and in a short time we were homeward bound as fast as the iron horse could carry us. The conductor very soon appeared. My heart began to swell with emotions of fear. What if he should not allow me to ride for half-fare? Before he got to me I stood up, and when he came with the shout, Tickets! I almost gave way under the feeling of depression. "Sir, I hope you will be kind enough to let me go for half-fare." "How far are you going?" he said, with a cheerful voice and smiling face, for he saw my perturbation. "To Shipman, sir." "And so you want to go to Shipman for half-fare do you?" "Yes sir." Taking the proffered sum he answered good-humoredly, "You may go for this," and passed on. You can, dear reader, better imagine my joy than I can tell it.

The next day about 11 o'clock, A. M., we arrived at the station of Shipman. With all possible haste we started for the house, one-half mile distant from the village. We met Cyrus and Lenard in the field at work. After congratulating them upon their good health, we started to the house, where we had the pleasure of meeting the light of home—father and mother, and the remaining members of the family. I shall not detain you, gentle reader, to tell you how glad we were to see each other, and how late we sat up that night, talking of the things which we had seen during the time we had been gone: suffice it to say we had a happy time.

During all this time the sore on my limb continued to sap my already waning strength. Occasionally a feeling

of joy would relieve me of the deep sadness under which
I almost daily went. Some times I felt perfectly resigned;
at others very impatient. All this feeling came as a natural consequence of the continued afflictions of my limb.
Often I would sit for hours, all the while my mind would
be filled with the most dismal forebodings. At length,
thanks to His name who doeth all things well, avenues
of usefulness opened to me, by which the monotony of
my afflicted life was relieved. The mind having been occupied with things of a LITTLE profit, but a GREAT DEAL
of pleasure, I felt much better, and could sing as the pat-
riarch Job, "I know that my Redeemer liveth;" though
surrounded with that which is calculated to dampen the
ardor of the most resolute, I felt that I was blessed above
thousands, and often would say to friends, who would be
pitying my condition. I thank God that it is no worse.

CHAPTER V.

ON THE ROAD OF PROGRESS.

Teacher of a School--The Throne of Grace my Standard--School
    Exhibition--Study of Latin--School-teaching at Ridge Prairie
    --A Discussion--Difficulties Overcome--My Call to the Minis-
    try—A Grand Celebration--On the "Grounds"--Adieu to
    "Hop Hollow"--Teaching at "the Ridge"--Full School--
    Measles--Death of Mary Blair and William Wilson--Grief.

GROWING weary of doing nothing, I immediatly resolved
to do SOMETHING, which, being put in execution, found me
comfortably situated in the beautiful little town of Jerseyville, the teacher of a flourishing school. I labored in this
capacity six months, during which time I added to my
stock of knowledge, by studing what I had not previously

known. It was about the first of January, 1860, that I started for the above mentioned town, for the sole purpose of trying to do something to aid me in gaining the wants of life, and also to relieve my mind from the monotony of doing nothing.

I went to my uncle P. S. Breeden and his wife Cordelia, both of whom were delighted to have me become the teacher of the day school in the Baptist church. A meeting was called. After a free expression of feeling by the friends interrested in the enterprise, I was duly elected as teacher of the village day school. With joy in my heart, and a prayer to almighty God for guidance, I entered upon the important and then new duties of a teacher. I erected a throne of grace on the first morning, around which all else was made to revolved, and which I kept up as long as I remained in that place. At the end of the first quarter an exhibition was given, in which the whole school participated. It was witnessed by a large assemblage of the citizens, both white and colored. The weekly paper of the place spoke in the most commendable terms of the progress of the scholars " under the efficient management of their worthy teacher, Mr. Magee." That little extract placed me before the world in a light in which I had never shone. The consequence was, I then held a position in the mind of the public, which naturally opened a more extended sphere for me to labor in. At the expiration of the second quarter, I left them amidst many solicitations by both parents and pupils to remain.

I may add, that, during my stay in Jerseyville, I imbibed a love for classic lore, from which I shall never recover until I have been to the font of ancient literature, and drunk deeply from the stream which has rendered so many minds fertile and strong. Prof. Davis agreed to teach me the rudiments of Latin if I would come to his residence, a distance of one mile from my boarding house. I went, was shown what I must get up for the recitation which would take place every other day — three times a week. I took the prescribed task with a mind red hot, with thirst for a drink from the font, which, to my understanding, was sealed. I did as well as I could have expected, considering the amount of labour I had to perform.

In 1832, I attended the Wood River Baptist Association, in which meeting I was greatly encouraged in my already strong belief in the efficacy of prayer. Among the delegates was Elder Emanuel Cartwright, a man of God, in whom I had the utmost confidence. Among other incidents related by him of the signal instances in which God had answered his prayer, was the following very interesting episode — I give it in his own language, as near as I can recollect the words: "I was attending a meeting held in the open air; and about the time I was ready to preach, a sudden thunder-cloud came up, such as you have often seen in the month of August. I prayed to my God: 'O Lord, be pleased to stay the clouds and the rain until the service is over.' The services were continued, and not a drop of rain fell during the service, but immediately after the benediction, by the time the people were in their tents, I never saw such a shower of rain as fell that day."

This narrative greatly encouraged me in my belief in the efficacy of prayer. That evening brother Cartwright and I, with a number of brethern, occupied the same room. Before I closed my eyes to sleep that night, I begged brother Cartwright to pray to God for my restoration to heath. He promised me that he would. After the association adjourned and the delegates went to their respective homes, I still had faith in the efficacy of prayer, and wrote a letter to

brother Cartwright, to remind him of his promise to pray
for my restoration. He did pray for it, and I thank God
that I am to-day a living monument of God's faithfulness,
and of the efficacy of prayer.

During my affliction Drs. M. W. Seamon and J. W. Tra-
bue, resident physicans in Shipman, were very kind to me,
and did all they could to alleviate my suffering, in trying
to arrest the progress of the disease. I shall ever hold
them in grateful remembrance for their kindness to me
during my dark night of affliction. May God spare them
to a long life of usefullness.

Time, with its rapid wing, brought me to the fall of 1861,
which found me at a settlement called Ridge Prairie.
Here I become the teacher of a large school of over forty
scholars. In that neighborhood are two churches, one Baptist and one Methodist, which were situated in two districts;
the consequence of this was a general discussion as to
which the teacher should locate himself in. Of course both
parties were anxious to share the benefits of my labour, to
go to either of which would offend the other. Here was
Daniel Wilkerson, the advocate for the upper district, in
which was located the Methodist church. To my right
stood R. Vanderburge, the advocate for it to be held in the
lower district, in which the Baptist church was situated.
Through the commanding eloquence of Mr. Vanderburge,
I agreed to teach in the lower district, in which was situated the Baptist church. This step put nearly all the Methodist brethern against me and the school, which greatly
depressed me for I had many dear friends in that denomination whom I dearly loved; not only as Christians, but as
old acquantances.

Time went on and with it the difficulties of the past wore
out, and success attended our school in so great a manner,

that I was obliged at times to give some of the smaller classes to some of the advanced pupils to teach. The fall and winter terms having been finished, the summer vacations ensued, during which time I remained at home, occupying my leasure moments in reviewing the various branches usually taught in common schools, that I might be more proficient by the time of the next commencement.

For a long time previous to the spring of 1860, I felt that God had called me to the work of preaching the gospel. I tried in every way to excuse myself to myself, but without feeling relieved from the constant impression on my mind that I had a work to do in preaching the gospel. These thoughts occupied my mind during my waking hours, and at closing day I felt the same dissatisfaction, on account of my failure to discharge what was evident to my mind to be God's will concerning me. Some times I would catch myself preaching away, while engaged in domestic duty about my father's house. One morning, while my mother and the rest of the family were engaged in milking the cows in the barn yard, some distance from the house, I was at the house washing the breakfast dishes, and during that time my mind was carried away out of myself, so that I was oblivious to everything, and when I came to myself, I was startled at my own voice. I was preaching at the top of my voice from the text "For the great day of His wrath is come, and who shall be able to stand." I was startled at myself, and ran out of the house to see if any body was within hearing distance. I could see no one near. And when mother came home, I asked her if she heard any one preaching that morning; she said she had not. She asked me why; I said: "Oh nothing;" for I was ashamed to tell her that I had been preaching to the empty dishes. I finally related my feelings to a brother, who gave me little

4

or no encouragement, and this put me back further than ever. About six months after this conversation, I spoke to Elder John Livingstone about the continued impression I had on my mind, from which I could not rest day nor night. Old father Livingstone, for thus we addressed him, gave me great encouragement, and said, "My son, this is a clear call to the work of the ministry, and you should obey the call of God without delay." I then made my wishes known to the church, and a time was set for me to preach my trial-sermon, which I did on the second Sunday in August, 1860. From that day to this I was relieved of my anxiety of mind about the work of preaching the gospel. From that day, too, I have been regaining my health —both spiritual and temporal. — "To obey is better than sacrifice."

On the first of August, according to previous announcement, a grand celebration took place at Hop Hollow. A company of us agreed to hire a hack in Edwardsville, to take us to the looked for place. The early morning found us bound for Edwardsville, a distance of five miles, in a two horse wagon. Having arrived at the city mentioned, we immediately changed the clumsy country wagon for a beautiful hack. A few minutes were spent by our dear friend Joseph Dority, in detaching and attaching the train, when, all being ready, we started for the noted place of the resort of excursionists. At an early hour we arrived in Upper Alton, where a large number of our people, in buggies, wagons, on horseback and on foot, joined the procession; further on we overtook numbers, whose joyful countenance betokened a happy heart, and whose eyes seemed to flash in view of the cause of their assembling, and in view of the distant prospect of a natal day, in which millions of their brethern should be born again—born from the womb of slavery into the bright day which beams with the rays of liberty, in every ray of which shone the living characters of the natural endowment of the human family — life, liberty and the pursuit of happiness. We read in the distance, upon the folds of the banner of mercy, which was being fanned by the breeze of heaven, the inscription which engaged the wondering gaze of angels, and the compassion of the eternal God, the condescension of our Lord and Saviour Jesus Christ—Life. Let us thank God for this guarantee, for without this, our existance would be miserable indeed. The faithful could see the lacerated (then bondmen) emerging from his awful sepulchre, with eyes upturned to God, his deliverer, hands outstreched to seize the proffered boon. Behold him, hard by the side of the flag of liberty, triumphantly shouting to his former oppressors, " You have drawn my heart's best blood with that of my fathers, mothers and children: but see! I bleed there no more, for God has sent his angels to bind up all these wounds which thou didst inflict in thy hellish fury." God did send his forked lightning to scatter the cruel oppressor, and to tell them in tones of thunder which continued to belch forth its terrible threatenings from the mouth of the cannon for four consecutive years.

At eleven o'clock we were on the ground, where we met a number of dear friends, some of whom we had not seen for years. After the usual greeting of friends, with many a warm press of the hand, and the quiet succession of questions and answers, we went to the riverside. Already the steam of the approaching steamer gave us notice of her near arrival. On nearing the shore, we discovered that it was indeed a steamer from St. Louis, Mo., which was well filled with happy pleasure seekers from that city. The vast crowd having debarked, removed in stately grandeur to the place prepared for the speakers. After the speeches had been delivered, the general preparation ensued for dispatching the many good things, in the shape of turkeys, chickens, pies, cakes, etc. Soon the gathering twilight bade us seek our homes, many of which were far remote. In a short time we had bidden adieu to the many pleasing scenes which were associated with our visit to Hop Hollow, and the celebration of the First of August.

In September, 1862, I resumed teaching my school in Ridge Prairie. This time I was hired by the trustees of the upper district. I opened my school in the little Methodist chapel, with about fifteen pupils. Additions were received until the number of forty or fifty scholars was reached. Everything seemed to be in the way of progress, which was evinced more and more by the eagerness, with which they sought the attainment of still higher subjects. All was well, until about the 10th of January, when the measles broke out, and so infected the school, that I thought it best to discontinue it. Many of my dear scholars never returned to their school on earth, but went to their Father in glory. I must mention two, whom I loved as I never loved children before, especially little Mary Blair, eldest daughter of Mr. Henry Blair, a wealthy farmer in Ridge Prairie. She was the best child I ever saw, and could learn faster and recite her lessons better, than any of the scholars. The disease took her while she was attending school. So anxious was she to learn, that no weather prevented her attending school. At length it was discovered that the disease had taken hold of her vitals with an unrelenting grasp, to which she succumbed after an illness of two weeks. I could not have wept more bitterly around the grave of an own dear relative than I did at the grave of dear little Mary Blair. The next who fell a victim to death from the same disease was little William Wilson, who was a dear little fellow, and passionately fond of his teacher. He was always prepared, when asked about any little misdemeanor, to tell the whole truth.

Soon after this I bade the pleasant associates of Ridge Prairie farewell, as the season of spring preparation was approaching. Often I advert to the scenes of my sojourn, as teacher of "the country school" with mingled feelings of joy and sadness, hoping for the happy day, when friend shall meet friend in the congregation of the blessed.

CHAPTER VI.

AN AWFUL TRIAL.

Limb Worse--Dr. Pope--Painful Examination--Death of the Bone --An Operation Necessary--Return to Wood River--Getting My Mind Composed--Living Near to God--Taking Leave of My Father's Family--Rev. J. H. Johnson--Steamer bound for St. Louis, Mo.--Reflections--Arrival at P. G. Wells--Consul-tation with Dr. Pope--The Day of Suffering--The Sisters' Hospital--The Doctor's Apartment--The Hour is Come--Nearer, My God, to Thee--Sensation--The Surgical Operation --Back to Consciousness--Start for My Boarding House--Dreadful Sickness--The Morning Brings Relief--Conversation --Meditation--Growing Better--A Few Words About Elder J. H Johnson--Ready to Go Home--Kind Friends.

TOWARDS the close of autumn of the year 1862, my limb grew worse. As the autumnal skies were dimmed with the smoke of the waning Indian summer, the leaves of the tall oak yielding his late rich foliage to the quickly approaching winter, so did the strength of my life begin to fade from the withering effects of the terrible disease from which I had suffered for many long dreary years. I found that something must be done to relieve my suffering or I must die. Having heard of a celebrated surgical doctor, Dr. Pope, of St. Louis, Mo., I went to see him on the 22nd of December.

Having made up my mind to meet the worst, I expected something very severe. He very closely examined the limb, probing it to the bone, which operation nearly made me faint, so great was the pain. I was informed by the doctor that whatever might have been the first cause, it was now a bad case of necrosis, or death of the bone, and that an operation would have to be performed in order to take away the dead portion of bone. As might have been expected, this announcement filled me with unmitigated terror. I returned home, thence to Wood River, where I had been teaching school since the beginning of September. I told my dear pastor, Elder J. H. Johnson, what doctor Pope had said. He expressed his usual sympathy, with the hope that I might survive the operation. Sister Johnson, his wife, told me that her husband should accompany me, when I got ready to go down to have the operation performed. I concluded that I would not have the operation performed until the expiration of the spring term. It took all that time to get my mind reconciled to submit to the operation.

During that time I lived very near the throne of grace, for I was uncertain as to the result of so dreadful an undertaking. Many had died from the severity of operations, the same which I must soon submit too, not knowing whether I should live through it or not. Towards the close of the school, I began to make preparations to start. I went home to see my father's family, and to tell them good-by for perhaps the last time. I could tell all farewell but my dear mother, whose heart was too full, in view of the eventful future. Ah! dear mother, I appreciate thy loving kindness, and will never forget the obligations of a son to a mother. Young men, be kind to your mothers, for not many know the depth of a mother's love; it is strong as death and as constant as the sun.

With tears freely flowing and heart anxiously beating, I took a long, long look at the house and home of my kindred dear, for, as far as I knew, the last time. Very soon I was borne at a rapid rate to Wood River, a distance of sixteen miles, to the residence of Rev. J. H. Johnson, at whose house I remained till next morning. Early in the morning Elder Johnson, his son, J. P. Johnson, and I were ready to start to Alton, from which place to take the steamer for St. Louis. In a short time we were comfortably situated on the beautiful steamer B. M. Runyan, bound for St. Louis. It was a beautiful day, it being the last day, of March; the trees were in their full livery of green; the birds sang sweetly their morning lay; nature seemed to be in a state of silent serenity. All of this had a tendency to awaken emotions of joy and sadness. As we glided down the placid waters of the Mississippi, I took a silent, long look at the beautiful trees on either side of the river, saying within, "Shall I ever behold this again?" An hour and a half having elapsed, we found ourselves at the wharf of the Alton and St. Louis Packet Company. We were met by Mr. Cunningham, who drove us to 33 Gay street, St. Louis, to the residence of Elder J. R. Anderson, who had secured me a boarding place at the residence of Mr. P. G. Wells, at No. 56 Gay street.

We were ushered in by brother Anderson, and introduced to Mr. and Mrs. Wells in his usual affable manner. Having been made welcome by our worthy friends, Mr. Wells and his wife, we began to ask about the doctor whom

I had come to see. After dinner we went to the doctor's residence on the corner of Tenth and Locust. I informed him that it was I who came to see him in the winter. He told me in a very few words to come the next morning to the Sister's Hospital, where he would attend to my case. I left his house with a heavy heart.

On the morning of the 1st of April, 1863, I went, in company with Elder Johnson and Mr. Wells, to the place assigned. On the way I almost sunk under the pressure of what I had not yet experienced. Several times I thought it a matter of impossibility for me to walk to the hack stand. At length we arrived at the stand, procured a hack, and started to the place of operation. In a short time we were in front of a splendid, large brick building—this is the Sisters of Charity Hospital. With every limb shaking I descended from the hack and went to the door, where we were meet my one of the singularly-dressed Sisters of that institution. On asking to be shown the way to Dr. Pope's apartment, she kindly led the way to a stairway, saying, "His room is in the third story." Up we went until we reached the room in question, when to my great astonishment the room was filled with students and patients (Dr. Pope is president of a large medical college). The time soon came for me to place myself on the long table made for the purpose of performing operations. I was told in a commanding tone to get ready, and place myself on the table. This so terrified me that I could not collect myself sufficient for some time to make the needed preparation. Some of the physicians attempted to help me, which broke the stupor into which I had fallen. I placed myself on the table, the doctor began to probe my limb, I began to scream, from pain, he cried: "give him the chloroform!" A towel was saturated with that fluid, and placed firmly over my face, being told to shut my eyes, and breathe hard and deep. I called brother Johnson, and took hold of his hand, asking him to stand by me, thinking that if I could only hold his hand during the operation I should be able to stand it. The table was ordered to be turned around, which disconnected us. Immediately the table was surrounded by twenty or thirty doctors. In the meantime Elder Johnson made his way through the crowd to my head, where he stood with one hand on my head and the other on my heart. The doctors told me repeatedly to shut my eyes, which I did not heed, until being told by Elder Johnson, my earthly safe-guard, I shut them.

After a short time I felt the drug had taken effect by the peculiar sensation which I experienced. I felt like I often have thought I shall feel when dying—a going away into another state—my mind becoming lighter—confused sounds, like the ringing of little bells was heard: a feeling of great quietude stole over my mind. I heard one of the doctors say, "Did you eat a hearty breakfast this morning?" I did not answer. He asked again, to which I answered, "Yes" I heard them say, "Give him some more chloroform," for the doctors had already begun to make the incision, as I was afterward informed by brethern Johnson and Wells. While the operation was being performed, a doctor held each of my wrists, with watch in hand to see how I was doing. At one time, while the doctor was cutting away, I involuntarily withdrew my left hand from the doctor, who held it, and thrust it to the place where the doctor was cutting. This was caused by some kind of sympathy, for I was wholly insensible of any pain.

At last the incision was made, the portion of dead bone discovered, the forceps applied, and a portion of decayed

5

bone drawn out. But there was a piece of bone, which seemed unyielding, to remove which the doctor had to take a small chisel and hammer, and break it to pieces, before he could remove it. You will doubtless be astonished when I tell you that to all this I was insensible. At the expiration of thirty minutes it was all done, the limb bound up, and many of the doctors preparing to leave. About the time most of the doctors had gone, I awoke as it were from a deep sleep. I looked around and saw the doctor replacing his lancets, knives, etc. I felt exceedingly happy, happy to know that I had survived the terrible operation. I raised up, and with my hand extended to the doctor, I grasped his hand and said: "The Lord will bless you for this." Some of the students asked: "How do you feel?" to which I answered, "I feel happy." I really meant what I said, for I was indeed happy. During the time of the operation, they said, I was singing and talking, preaching and praying.

All things having been made ready, we prepared to go to the carriage. I walked down the three flights of stairs unassisted, notwithstanding that eighteen pieces of bone had just been taken out of my limb. Arriving at my boarding house on Gay street, I was assisted to the fire, where I sat only a few minutes, when I got dreadful sick. In haste I was assisted to my room. That night I thought I should have died before morning, so great were the pains, that it was impossible to restrain myself from tossing from one side of the bed to the other, mad with pain. Brother Johnson was in the room, but he was so troubled that he could not rest. Often I heard him sigh deeply, and walk hurriedly up and down the floor, as one in great distress of mind. Towards morning the pain, like the shadows of night before the rays of the morning sun, began to withdraw itself. I awoke into full consciousness about four o'clock in the morning, when I called him to come and lie down, for he was sitting close to the grate of smouldering coals. The dim light of the still burning lamp lent a peculiar mellow appearance to the whole room. I began to converse with brother Johnson about the sufferings which I had endured during the night, and about what time I began to feel better. He answered and said to me: "About the time of your great sufferings, I earnestly prayed to the Lord to relieve you of your sufferings. I thought, what, if you should die before morning, far away from your relatives. While these thoughts were revolving in my mind, a thought came to me to try the strength of prayer, which I did, and I thank God that he has heard me."

The busy throng of the great city had begun to awake into activity. We turned our conversion to the scenes of terror which are enacted under the cover of night in great cities, saying that a few moments ago the great city was sleeping, now it is the great city awaking, fitting type of the judgment of the great day, when millions of beings shall be called to awake from the sleep of death unto the resurrection. The righteous shall be as a great city awaking into life and immortality; but the wicked shall be as were the great cities of Sodom and Gomorrah, awaking only to find that every righteous lot has been taken by cherubic legions to mansions in glory. Thus passed the few hours before the family arose. Though I had suffered so greatly during the night, I felt in the morning to be the subject of peculiar blessing. Oh blessed Jesus! thou from whom cometh light, life, and salvation, thou dost regard the afflicted poor, and in tender compassion, dost bind up the broken in heart, and heal their wounds. O my eternal God, may I always see mercy in the dispensations of thy providence, that when thou liftest the rod it be tempered with mercy, and that when thou smitest, thou smitest to heal.

I continued to grow better and better until I was able to rise without being assisted. Elder Johnson remained until he saw that I was out of danger; then he went home. Dear reader, permit me to turn aside from the subject of this narrative to say a few words about Elder J. H. Johnson, who was so solicitous about my welfare. He was the one who baptized me, and who had often given me encouragement in preaching the gospel. He was a man whom every one loved that knew him. Always ready to give a word of consolation to the dejected. He has since gone to his rest. Though gone he is not forgotten, for his work is still following him, and I dare say will continue to go on, to bless many that are yet unborn.

On the 10th of April I was so far recovered as to be able to go home. I found my brother, A. S. Magee, who, having come to St. Louis on business, was a great help in assisting me to get home. I must not forget to mention the kindness with which I was treated by Mr. and Mrs. Wells, and many of the friends who kindly visited me. Brother Thos. Reasoner deserves special mention for the kind attention which he gave me in dressing my wound every day as long as I stayed in St. Louis. May Heaven bless all who in any way administered to my necessity.

CHAPTER VII.

THE MORNING COMETH.

NIGHT is the emblem of sorrow and trouble; the time when all things that would captivate the mind, are wrapt in sable gloom; it is then that many an anxious mother sits at the bed side of her sick son, daughter, or husband, waiting for the coming day. Night precedes the day; it may be long and dark, but it has a morning when the rising dawn pales the night, the shout of the morning resounds from east to west, which is taken up by ten thousand voices in nature, all of which proclaim—the morning cometh. The soul, by sin oppressed, falls at the foot of the cross, and with blinded eyes cries, "What must I do to be saved." Faith points him with her radiant finger to the cross; and when he beholds him who died upon it for his salvation, he feels the sun of righteousness rising in his soul, chasing away the night of death and the shadows of unbelief. The morning has come; the poor child of affliction, amid the pangs of dark despair, often cries out in the anguish of mind and body, "when shall the morning come." Hope tells him of a medicine yet untried, which will have the effect to break the spell of the night of suffering. With joyful haste he reaches forth the hand of his confidence, to take the proffered aid, which comes in the light of hope, but

returns in the garb of despair. Thus disappointment suc-
ceeds disappointment, till hope, the silver-winged messen-
ger that comes to all, seems to have taken its final flight.
Man's extremity is often God's opportunity. When self
has worked itself clear out of self, then He who is mighty
to save interposes to bring the wanted object. I know this
to have been so with me by that *best* of teachers—experi-
ance. For many years I tried everything that imagination
could concieve of, or that any person could tell of, and *all*
to no purpose. At last the Lord took me under *his* guidance, and by means of his appointment, gave me to hope
for better days to come. The time of my entire recovery is
not come, but, I believe it is in prospect. Already my
heart says, "The morning cometh." Yes, by the blessing
of God, the sore that is now daily saping my strength, shall
soon be healed thoroughly. May God speed the day
according to his own will. My soul shall rest in hope, and
sing as I pass through the mists of affliction—"The morning cometh."

At the meeting of the association in August, 1863, with
the Piasa church, I was offered for ordination. I was
closely examined by a committee of ministers, who, after
due deliberation, thought it advisable to consummate their
determination, by the laying on of hands on the following
Sunday. I was therefore publicly ordained to the work of
the ministry, on Sunday afternoon, between one and two
o'clock, in the presence of hundreds of spectators, both
white and colored. In the following September I was
called to the pastorate of Salem church, on Wood River, in
which capacity I labored for one year. In October, by the
blessing of God, we began a series of meetings, which were
abundantly blessed of God, in the conversion of 15 or 16
souls. Many old backsliders were reclaimed. The church

was in a blaze of prosperity. The meeting continued three weeks. Every night the church was filled to its greatest capacity, many were obliged to remain out doors. In November we visited the baptismal waters twice. The first time I immersed nine in the name of the Holy Trinity. The second time I immersed five. The scene was one of great interest, it being witnessed by many from all parts of the surrounding country. I will mention here, that two of those whom I immersed were sons of the late Rev. J. H. Johnson, one of whom I am happy to state has begun to preach Jesus. Some of those who were then baptized are gone to their rest in glory. They have fought the good fight of faith, and are now at their rest—the rest prepared for the people of God. Immediately after this I was called to take the oversight of Piasa Church, in supplying them with preaching and breaking of bread once in every month. I accepted and labored with much acceptance as long as I remained in the country. In the spring of 1864 I went to meet a called convention in St. Louis, Mo. There I met Elder Troy, of Canada West, with whom I had much conversation about the *one* object of my desire—education. Finding him to be a man of more than ordinary intelligence, and that he was of the same mind as I in regard to education, I therefore unhesitatingly unbosomed myself to him with regard to my longing desire for an opportunity of finishing my education in all its departments. We separated, but did not forget each other, as will be seen hereafter. During the summer my health began to grow worse, and it struck my mind, that a northern climate would be much better for my health than that in which I then lived. Therefore I wrote a full letter to Elder Troy, telling him of my failing health, and asking him if he could secure for me a situation as a teacher in the Windsor colored school,

at the same time telling him of the approaching association, which was to take place in Jacksonville, saying that I
would be pleased to see him there. We met, but without
affecting anything, for the school was supplied, and the
church was expecting Elder Sneethen to take the pastorate,
or I could have had the pastoral charge of it.

Time passed on and still my thirst for learning increased.
I happened to think of a plan by which I thought I should
be able to facilitate the obtaining of the much wanted tres-
ure. I went to St. Louis and laid the plan before my friend
Mr. Wells. It was this:—to get my life insured for two
thousand dollars, and put the policy in the hands of some
good man, who would let me have a few hundred dollars to
finish my education. I went down to the insurance office
and told the agent my intentions; he told me it would be
a capital idea, and that I could give no better security.
The next thing to be done, before preceeding any further,
was to find that *good* man, who would take the policy, and
lend me the required amount to support me two years at
school. He could not be found, and the consequence was
a dashing of my fair prospects to the ground. Friends, you
may learn from this how great was my desire for knowledge
—that I was willing to pawn the insurance policy of my
life to obtain it.

In October, 1864, I was called to the pastorate of the
Baptist church, in Springfield, Illinois, and accepted; but
owing to the unwillingness of their former pastor to give
up what he claimed, his right to a refusal, I handed in my
resignation. In the mean time I received a letter from
Elder Troy, stating that he had been to the city of Toronto,
and that the Baptist church of that place had authorized
him to get them a minister, and that he wanted me to go
immediately to the city of Toronto, C. W. That he would

meet me at a little town called Atlanta, at which time he
would tell me more about it. We duly met, arrangements
were made as to the probable best course for me to pursue.
My mind told me that Toronto was the place for me.

Prospects began to brighten in regard to the opportunities of learning which I had so long sought. I asked many
questions about the churches, institutions of learning, and
the situation of the city. The answers brought me the most
complete satisfaction. Ere we parted my mind was filled
with visions bright, in which I felt myself hastening with
eager steps to the vast fields of learning, the amply filled
chapel with attentive, devout worshipers. I remained with
Elder Troy about one week, stopping at the various cities
and towns, in which he exhibited his very excellent panorama Having made all preparations neccessary for starting for the far famed shores of Canada, I was informed
that my little brother Lenard had been persuaded to leave
his home, to go into the army as a substitute for one of our
neighbors. The dastardly act was accomplished by this
man, whose name I will not mention, and his accomplices.
This event nearly distracted my aged mother, in so much,
that she appeared completely overcome with grief. Her
grief was aggravated by the taunting remarks of the poor
cowards, that "it does not make any difference, it is only
a nigger." This shows how much wickedness and coward-
ice they were possessed of. He feared to go himself; he
was also an inveterate hater of our race, who were not good
enough to go to the common schools in his sight; but the
nigger was plenty good to be shot at instead of the white
man. I immediatly told mother that I would accompany
her, and assist in getting him out of the army, for he had
already gone without getting his promised money, which
was only two hundred and twenty five dollars. The next

morning found us on board the cars, bound for Springfield, Illinois. On arriving there, we went to our good friend, Mr. Jackson, preparatory to going to the Govenor to try to get my brother released. We went to his excellency, the Govenor, and found that the disposition of those matters rested solely with the war-department, that we should go to some General in the city, who would tell us what to do. We went to him, and related the circumstances of the case; he referred us to another General out at camp Butler, about five miles distant from the city. Then we had to go to Jacksonville, the place where he was enlisted, to get more particulars respecting it. After this we were referred back to camp Butler. All appeared to be against the probability of securing his release. He had been examined and returned to the camp as being fit for the service. Just as we were turning to take leave of the camp, with hearts big with grief, my attention was directed to a very gentlemanly looking person, whom my mother addressed: "Sir, my son was persuaded to run away from home to join the army; he went without my consent; he is also under age, and I fear his strength is not sufficient for the task of a soldier." "How old is your son?" asked the General. "Fourteen, sir." "I will have him sent for, madame, and if after his examination again there is any chance for him he shall be released." He was sent for and was again brought before the army physicans. While he was being examined, I breathed a silent pray to Him who holds the reins of universal government for the release of my brother for my dear mother's sake. My mother stood near me in a pensive mood, doubtless sending a prayer to God, with that fervor, such as a mother alone can command. In a few minutes the General appeared, saying: "Your son is dismissed, and will be home in a few days." It is impossible for me to attempt a description of my mother's deep heart-felt joy, which could only be expressed with tears, which were freely shed. I remained in Springfield until his papers were made out, when I brought him home.

I am constrained to say, "The Lord is my refuge and strength, a very present help in trouble."

CHAPTER VIII.

CANADIAN PROSPECTS.

Christmas at Home--My Mother's Joy--New-Year's Day--On My Way to Canada--Toronto--The Church--Sabbath School--First Sabbath in that Pulpit--Called--A Series of Meetings--Great Revival--Baptismal Scene--Large Audience--Living for Jesus--Study of Latin--Home on a Visit--Alton and St. Louis--First of August Celebration--Springfield, Illinois--Funeral of Wm. H. Magee--A Letter to the Church--Rev. De Baptiste--Windsor--British Soil--Baptist Church in Detroit--Baptist Church in Windsor--Home again--Library burned.

CHRISTMAS-DAY came, and with it the usual happy greet ings. Again the whole family were gathered around the christmas dinner save two, one was far to the west, amid the scenes of the Rocky Mountains, in quest of the fleeting treasures of earth. The other was fifteen miles distant, among the festivities of his own happy home. Robert, my nephew, had just returned home from the war, on a sixty days' furlough. Mother, as usual, had spared no pains to make home and all connected with it happy. It was her chief delight to have "her boys" around her at least once a year, that she might have an opportunity of showing, in various ways, her appreciation of that for which she alone wished to live—her family. During the day, and especially at dinner, my heart was filled with sadness, when my mother addressed me and my brother:—" We are here together this Christmas, but the Lord only knows where we shall be the next." It must be remembered that my brother Cyrus was coming with me to go to school. New year's day came with its gladdening scenes, but it brought no joy to me, for my thoughts were occupied with the present and the immediate future.

On Wednesday, the 17th of January, 1865, we started for Springfield en route for Canada, touching at Chicago and Detroit. At the latter place, we took the Grand Trunk for Toronto, arriving at about nine o'clock at Saturday night the 20th. Having been directed by Elder D. W. Anderson, to go to Mrs. Hollins, in Queen street, on arriving we told the cabman to drive us there, to which he responded by placing us snugly in his sleigh (for the snow was deep) among the heavy buffalo robes, with which he was well provided. Away we went, at a rapid rate, to the place where I had never been before. In a few minutes we were ushered into the residence of Mrs. Hollins, but finding there was no one there but a few young men and women (for Mrs. Hollins had retired), I thought I had better go down to the shop, where Mr. Hollins was; so suiting the action to the thought, we engaged the driver to take us there. We found the deacon, a very affable old gentleman, and passed the evening very pleasantly. Next morning being Sunday, I was anxious to see the church. After breakfast, we went to Sabbath school, where we found quite an agreeable propect, under the superintendency of Mr. R. Thomas. I was very much pleased with the chapel, but a little disappointed with the congregation, as it was rather small—a common thing, I afterwards learned, in the morning. In the afternoon every thing was much more interesting, congregation larger, singing better, and every body seemed to be "in the Spirit on the Lord's day." Every body's attention seemed to have been turned to me—I mean their ocular attention. I could frequently hear whispers from all sides:—" I wonder if that is the minister?"

The service being concluded, I was introduced to a great many of the brethren, whom I found to be of the most amiable character, and I am proud to say that opinion has been sustained to the present day, and, if any thing, many have shown themselves more and more benevolent. I never saw a lot of people, who seemed to be more willing to do what is right, than did these people—indeed, they were exemplary.

The next Sunday was the time for me to appear before the congregation, to be judged by them as to whether they would choose me as their pastor. I was perfectly indifferent about making any special preparation for the occasion, trusting in the Lord, as I always try to do, for guidance. I took my text in the morning from the Psalms:—" The Lord has done great things for us, whereof we are glad.." I treated it in two ways—temporal and spiritual. In the former part I adverted to the great things the Lord has done for the whole race of man. But I referred particularly to what great things the Lord has done for us as a race, in lifting us from the horrible pit of slavery to the rock of sweet liberty. In the afternoon I preached from the Psalms lxxxiv. 11:—" For the Lord God is a sun and shield, etc."

I continued to fill the desk from that time until I was permanently called to the pastorate, which took place on the 7th of February, 1865.

Immediately after my arrival, we began a series of meetings at brother Tom Williams, in Agnes street. The in-

terest continued until the house was so densly crowded, as
to demand a removal of the meetings to a more commo
dious room.   Having been solicited, I took the responsibility of removing the meeting to the chapel.   At first, the
congregation was very meagre, but when the Holy Spirit
began to stir up the old Christians, the light began to burn
so bright, that the influence of its hallowed beams began
to spread far and wide, until the chapel was crowed every
night with both white and colored people, seemingly from
every quarter.

To enter into a minute description of that great out-
pouring of God's Spirit, would defy the descriptive power
of the most powerful intellect.   Every evening at half past
seven o'clock, the chapel would be so crowded, that it was
very difficult to find room for the many that were earnestly seeking the salvation of their souls.   As the
meeting grew older the interest waxed stronger, and the
Holy Spirit began to do the work of regeneration.   Some
nights as many as five or six would rise, telling the glad
news that the Lord had done all things well.   Some were
converted after they had left the chapel for the evening.
Sister Hollins house was a great gospel hospital, which
was crowded with anxious inquirers daily while the meetings continued.   One lady was so powerfully wrought
upon that she could not come from the place where she
was sitting about mid way of the chapel.   She was
brought forward to the anxious seat, where she lay for
some time, cold and motionless, apparently dead.   But
when the fire from Heaven came, and God from glory
spoke peace to her soul, she arose from there, telling the
news in loud hallelujahs.   This glorious feast lasted nearly
eight weeks.

The next scene of interest took place at the baptismal

font, in the baptistry of the Rev. Dr. Caldicott, pastor of the Bond Street Baptist church. The first baptizing took place on the evening of the first of March, at which time I immersed twenty willing, happy souls in the name of the Father, and in the name of the Son, and in the name of the Holy Ghost. The Dr. had given notice from his pulpit on the Sunday previous that a baptizing of members into the fellowship of the Queen Street Baptist Church would take place on the following Wednesday evening. Long before we got ready to begin the exercises, the house was densely crowded, there being fifteen hundred persons present. I spoke briefly from John x. 9:—"I am the door." I had never before spoken to so large a congregation, therefore I felt a little intimidated, until the Holy Spirit came to my assistance. After the sermon, the candidates repaired to the room immediately in the rear of the pulpit, there being a nice arrangement for the female candidates to come through a door under the platform of the pulpit, but so ingeniously arranged as to appear to come through the pulpit.

The second baptizing took place on the 16th of the same month, in the presence of a large audience. This time we baptized sixteen. That and the previous baptizing constituted the most happy periods of my life. The light of the Saviour's countenance seems to have shone upon my pathway for months afterward, insomuch that I seldom entered the sacred desk without feeling the Saviour nigh, aiding me in the ministration of the word. I could wish to have remained in such a frame as that, then the duty of preaching the gospel would be all my theme. I have reason to thank God for the continuation of his goodness in permitting me to feel a goodly degree of the power of the Spirit, whenever I attempt to speak in his name.

Since that time, some of those whom I baptized have gone to their rest, they having fought the good fight, which was of short duration, have laid down the weapons of their warfare, the last enemy being conquered—faith and hope being exchanged for the fruition of heaven.

Not wishing to lose any time, and desiring to reap the golden harvest for which the sickle of the mind had grown rusty in waiting, and to facilitate this operation, I engaged the services of Mr. Chas. E. Cummings, a former student of the Toronto Grammar School, to teach me the Latin, until such time as my pastoral duties would permit me to enter some of the very excellent high schools of the city. He was engaged for three months, but before the expiration of that time he took a notion to go to St. Louis, for the purpose of teaching school; he, however, supplied his place by a Mr. Alfred Baker, student of the Grammar School. I continued under his teaching three months, then I went home on a six weeks visit, to see my friends, and father, mother, brothers, and sisters. I left the city of Toronto on the 10th day of July, 1865, for home, arriving there on the 12th, found all well, except my mother, who was greatly afflicted by a fall from a cherrytree, which she had climbed for the purpose of gathering cherries. By the goodness of God, she was permitted to get much better before I left for my field of labor. In about a week after arriving home, I went to see my old friend, Elder W. W. Stewart. It being late in the evening when I got there, the family had retired. But a loud knock brought the reverend gentleman to the door, who was as much surprised to see me as he would have been had one risen from death. I preached for him the next Sunday, and Monday morning found me on board the cars, bound for St. Louis, Missouri. I went to the residence of Elder

Livingstone, where I was very soon followed by my esteemed friend Chas. Cummings. In the afternoon of the next day, I visited, with much pleasure, the school of which Mr. Cummings and Miss Stanly were the teachers. I was very much pleased to see the large number of adults and children, who hitherto had been, by the curse of slavery, prohibited the privileges of even learning to read that best of books—the Bible.

On the 1st day of August the citizens of St. Louis collected together at Uhrig's Cave, to celebrate that day, in honer of the manumission of the state of Missouri. Flaming bills announced to the public that the following gentlemen would address the audience:—Rev. J. H. Magee, of Toronto, Rev. Mr. Young, of New York, and Rev. Mr. Brooks, of St. Louis. The hour for commencement having arrived, the spacious hall of Uhrig's Cave was filled with patriotic citizens, whose bodies, to a goodly number, were recently manacled with the cruel chains of slavery. The tongue that was wont to shout the battle cry of freedom, was hushed by the uplifted lash and the ever present slave pen. The heart of many a fair one, which in time of slavery was awakened by the tender passion—love, was frozen into solitude and discontent at the thought of that power, which could separate at any moment, two hearts which God had joined together in the indissoluble ties of eternal affection. The scene of abject bondage having been changed for one of partial liberty, I say partial, because that is not LIBERTY which denies a part of the citizens of a country rights which others are invited to enjoy. The hearts of many were filled with joys before unknown. The mother was there with her babes, whom she now looked upon as being her own; she had no fear that perhaps ere the morning's sun tinged the eastern sky, the

6

flowers of her youth, the children of her bosom, would be torn from her, to be exchanged for gold. Now the charter of liberty, which had been signed by a noble man—Abraham Lincoln—was ratified by Heaven, and the angels doubtless sang the triumphs of liberty in the never dying hallalujahs, such as went up to heaven when Babylon was fallen. There was the young wife, trusting confidingly in the manly person at her side, there being no dismal forebodings as to a probable separation, until God, who their being gave would take them with himself to live. The lover was there with his loved one at his side, his heart filled with the gladdening prospects of an auspicious future, with no fears that before the nuptial tie could be celebrated they might be torn asunder by the unrelenting hand of slavery's votary.

During the speeches the appreciation of what was said was frequently evinced by the hearty outbursts of vociferous cheers. Towards evening the vast assemblage dispersed, feeling very grateful for having been permitted to participate in the celebration of the day of glorious liberty.

I returned home to remain a week before starting to the association in Springfield, Illinois. On arriving at Miles Station, I met my mother, who handed me a letter, containing the sad intelligence of the death of my brother, W. H. Magee. He seemed to have died from the effects of a gun shot wound, which he received accidently, while crossing the plains. This sad intelligence brought new grief to my heart, which, added to that of leaving my afflicted mother, made me feel exceedingly sorry. I went home and enjoyed its hospitalities with as much pleasure as I could under the circumstances, until the day came for me to start to Springfield, Illinois. On Thursday I took leave of mother, father, and the family, for Springfield, and thence to my church in Toronto. We had a most delightful session; means were concerted for the general good of Zion, and for the uplifting of our race. A noble article was written by the Rev. Mr. Poindexter of Ohio, "On the State of the Country," in which he traced what would be the inevitable results of emancipation, without the privileges of exercising the rights of citizens in maintaining that blessed boon. At this meeting the funeral sermon of my brother was preached by Elders R. J. Robinson and Samuel Livingstone. It was a solemn occasion— one which caused the shedding of many tears for one who in life was deeply interested in the affairs of the church and ministerial elevation. He had spent a great deal of his time, after he had faithfully served his minority at home, in the acquisition of knowledge. He went first to Racine, and spent some time there in a lightning rod factory, studying during intermissions that would occur. Finding it rather hard to work and study at the same time, he resolved to take what means he had accumulated, and respair to the celebrated seat of learning—Oberlin College. He remained there over two years, when necessity compelled his removal.

He next wrote to the principal of Athens College in Ohio, stating his embarrassments, and his calling, and how he had striven to obtain a thorough education, that he might be able to go and preach the word with humble boldness, having studied to show himself a workman that needeth not to be ashamed. The president kindly gave him the privilege of attending his college free of charge, and he gladly accepted the proposal, remaining in that institution until he felt it his duty to prepare to do something else. He then removed to Cincinnati, and engaged himself to

work in an Italian marble factory. Finding that he could
not get on the road to affluence fast enough, he resolved to
go with a company then getting up to the gold mines of
the far west, from whence the painful news of his death
came to us. It is just to say that he was a most exemplary and devoted christian. Below I will give a copy of a
letter from him to his church at Piasa, Macoupin County,
Illinois.

BLACK HAWK, Aug. 25. 1863.

DEAR BRETHREN IN THE LORD:

I now hasten to transmit to you a few lines, to let you
know that through the mercies and blessings of God my
health is good. I arrived here safely a few days ago. The
reason that I did not write you while I was in the northern
mines, was from lack of communication by mail. On my
gold excursion I found both gold and quicksilver, but it is
wholly impossible for any man to mine successfully in that
region, unless he belongs to a large party and well guarded
against the Indians. That country is a very rich gold
mining country throughout its whole extent—and there
have been some very rich discoveries in the British posses-
sions, at St. Mary's Lake, Moosehead Lake, and Carribro;
at Deer Lodge, on Gold creek, they were making from
sixty to sixty five dollars per day to the man. Bannock
City is surrounded by rich mines. About the time we got
ready to work, the Indians discovered us—they numbered
about forty, and were well armed and drilled. There were
only eight of us, therefore we were obliged to evacuate.
They shot at me four times, one of the balls grazing my
wrist. One man was shot through two coats, two shirts,
and vest, the ball leaving a blister on his breast; another
had the wast-bands of his pantaloons shot off; and one

man had the top of his head grazed. On our way to Pike's Peak, we were captured by over three hundred Sioux—being a portion of the tribe that committed the outrages in Minnesota. They were bent upon killing us, but as God would have it, there happened to be three friendly Indians among them, who knew one of our party; by their intercessions we were released. We were surrounded by them; they had their guns charged and primed. Had their been one careless one among them, to have burst a cap, or fired, then would have the brutal slaughter begun. There would not have been one left to have told the lamentable narrative. I then, brethern, thought of you all, and the sacred desk of God. I also remembered the old proverb, that "the way of the transgressor is hard." Brethern, I do beg an interest in your prayers to God in my behalf. While traveling and wandering through this wild wilderness, and over the rocky cliff I still felt that God was mine, and that I was his—I still felt his protecting care over me.

Brethren, whenever I fall, whether it be on the plains or in the wild desert, I expect, through the assistance of God, by the grace already given, to make heaven my home, where the cracking of the Indian's rifle and his war whoop shall be heard no more, and where sin and death shall never enter; where the weary soul shall rest from its labor; where parting shall be no more, nor Sabbath ever end, nor the congregation ever break up. Oh, praise ye the Lord, praise ye him from whom all blessing flow, for his mercies and his watchful protecting care over us. He has preserved us through dangers, both seen and unseen.

Brethren, keep your heads above the waves, because the storm will soon be over, and then, if we have been faithful to the end, we shall moor our frail barks safely in the harbor, and be housed in eternal heaven, to join with the angels

in one perpetual strain of joy around the mediatorial seat
of Christ.

I now close, hoping, by the mercies of God, to hear from
you soon.   I remain, yours truly in the Lord,

W. H. MAGEE.

At the close of the associations each delegate sought his
respective home. I took leave of my many friends on Monday evening, after the greater part of my friends living
south of Springfield had taken leave of their friends, and
gone by the morning train. I arrived in Chicago early
Tuesday morning, and found my way to the hospitable residence of the Rev. R. De Baptiste, in Fourth Avenue.
Having partaken of the hospitalities of our esteemed brother, we went to the various streets of interest with which
the metropolis abounds.

I met Elder Poindexter, of Columbus, Ohio, in the city;
and finding that he and his wife were going to start home
over the Michigan Southern railroad, I also concluded to
start on the same evening and by the same road for Detroit
The hour of starting having come, we went to the depot
whence the Michigan Southern train stood, with steam
ascending high, ready to start. The train was densely
crowded, there not being room in the cars to obtain a single
seat. This, however, was very soon remedied by the at-
tachment of more cars. In a few minutes we were speed-
ing away as fast as steam could carry us, leaving the beautiful city of Chicago among the things of the PAST. On
the morning following I arrived at the city of Detroit, from
thence I took the ferry boat "Windsor" for the town of
Windsor, Canada West. Although an American born subject, I must confess that I felt more at home the very first
time my feet ever trode upon British soil than I ever felt

in America. This is from some unaccountable reason. I
went in the first place to Mr. J. W. Brown, a good old
baptist friend; here I met Mrs. Brooks, wife of the Rev. W.
P. Brooks of St. Louis; being old acquaintances, we passed
the time very agreeably. I met Elder Troy at home, by
whom I was introduced to Elder Chase, pastor of the Baptist Church in Detroit. I called on the Elder in question,
received an appointment to preach in his church on Sabbath at three o'clock, P. M. I was very much pleased with
his church and congregation, it being furnished with a good
organ, at which a colored lady presided, showing a perfect
acquaintance with the excellent art of church music. In
the evening I was invited to preach in the spacious Baptist
Church of Windsor. I was welcomed by a fine apprecia-
tive audience; was very much pleased to see the progress
that MANY of our people were making in Windsor towards
affluance. Some, who, having escaped from slavery without a dollar, after paying their way to Canada, have fine
brick houses, stores, etc. Others have handsome frame
buildings. Let the traducer of the colored man, in whose
mouth the vile lie of negro incapacity rests, look at what
has been done in Windsor and elsewhere, after spending
the strength of his years in unrequited toil.

I next turned my steps homewards to my own charge in
Toronto. Arriving there about the last of August, I was
met with the sad news that Mrs. Hollins, the lady with
whom I boarded, had been burned out, and that all my
library had shared the same fate, and had perished in the
fire.

CHAPTER IX.

LIFE IN TORONTO.

Sad Intelligence—Sympathy—Colored Citizens—Funerel Sermon
of President Lincoln—The Sermon—Toronto Grammer School
—A Prize for Proficiency in Latin—Progress—Reminiscence
—Churches and Ministers—A Gospel-fortified City—Delight-
ing in the House of God—A glorious Hope--The Fruition of
Heaven--A Description--Affliction of Life--The Bond Street
Baptist Church--T. F. Caldicott, D. D.--Richmond Street
Wesleyan Church--Rev. Wm. Stepenson--Rev. Mr. Pollard--
The Elm Street Wesleyan Church--Mr. John Potts--Knox
Church—The Evangelical Union Church—Rev. Mr. Melville
—The Sayer Street B. M. E. Church—Rev. Peter Anderson--
The Queen Street Baptist Church--Rev. J. H. Magee.

ON the 14th day of April, the sad intelligence of the
assassination of the chief magistrate of the United States—
the venerated Abraham Lincoln—was borne to the quiet
city of Toronto. The city was a vast house of mourning.
Business on the day of his funeral was nearly all sus-
pended.

Most of the churches evinced their sympathy by opening
their doors on the day of his funeral, when vast crowds of
citizens went to the different churches to hear his funeral
preached by their respective pastors. The colored citizens
of Toronto showed their veneration for our much lamented
friend and benefactor, by calling a meeting of condolence,
to meet in the Queen Street Baptist Chapel, where, in the
presence of a crowded house, I had the mournful duty to
perform of preaching the funeral sermon of our great benefactor, whose name will be ever dear to generations yet
unborn.

I will give a general outline of the subject used on that
occasion: " Mark the perfect man, and behold the upright,

for the end of that man is peace." Psalms XXXVII. 37
The object of our coming together is one of the most solemn
in its nature that it has been our painful duty to witness.
It is to show the last tribute of respect to one of the most
illustrious men the world ever knew. The means by which
he came to an untimely end is the most tragical and inhu-
man that was ever perpetrated in a civilized world. It is
our purpose to recount in a very brief manner the life and
death of the noble and heroic statesman, Abraham Lincoln,
the father of the liberty of four million souls. We shall
consider the text as descriptive of the character of the
lamented late President of the United States. We shall
first notice A CHARACTER DESCRIBED "a perfect man." This
eminent man was born in Hardin County, Kentucky, on
the 12th of February 1809. His father and mother were
consistant members of the Baptist Church.

I. The character deeribed, "A perfect man," we can
say with the uttermost confidence of the late President.
" Mark the perfect man and behold the upright, for the end
of that man is peace." God is perfect in all his attributes.
He has a family in heaven, whom he has perfected in
Christ. His family on earth are in a state of progression,
destined to perfection in Christ, the Saviour of the world.
"And ye are complete in him, which is the head of all
principality and power." The Lord has opened a perfect
road to eternal rest, and commanded man to walk in that
road. It is evident that man must have attained to a certain stage of that principle in which the way was laid out
before he could be accepted as a traveler in the king's
highway. Having entered this glorious way, we are commanded to WALK in it. " Walk before me and be thou perfect," saith God. The whole object of the gospel is to
save a lost world. Nothing could have induced the son

7

of God to robe himself in humanity, to sojourn in the world, and finally die upon the cross, but that the world through him might be perfected. This Christ, whom the apostles preached, warning every man, and teaching very man in all wisdom, that they might present every man PERFECT in CHRIST JESUS. "Whereunto I also labor, striving according to his workings, which worketh in me mightily." This doctrine is further evident from a consideration of what is absolutely necessary before man can be a fit subject for the kingdom of heaven, viz. regeneration, or being born again. This operation is like unto a NEW creation. The old man and his deeds of imperfection have been exchanged for the new man—Christ Jesus. "If any man be in Christ, he is a new creature, old things are passed away, behold, all things are become new."

Again it is our privilege to have a PERFECT "love." We may have a PERFECT hope, which hope is founded on a perfect foundation. This perfect hope is in opposition to all that is false. Perfect love is in opposition to dissimulation. We may have perfect sentiments of right principles, for which the late President was pre-eminently noted, and to which every lover of justice, equality, and liberty will say of the subject of this discourse. "Mark the perfect man"— a man whom angels might admire, as in the steady course of duty he unswervingly ran. And when, as if with the spirit of inspiration, he took his pen to write the noble edict of emancipation, guided by the angel of justice, cheered on by the angel of mercy, encouraged by the God of heaven, animated by the groans of four millions of brethren, whose chained hands were raised imploringly to heaven, crying: "How long, O Lord, how long shall we remain in these bonds;" the news, methinks, was re-echoed from the heavenly world, as the word FOREVER FREE was ratified by the angel of justice, who, upon the wings of time, flew to glory, exclaiming: "Babylon is fallen!" Hear! the clanking chains of millions of hitherto bondmen falling down to oblivion. See! the tyrant slavery, bound by liberty, trembling down to hell! Listen! hear all the retinue of heaven shouting, hallelujah, salvation, and glory, and honor, and power unto our God. Why? For true and righteous are his judgments. True and righteous judgments. Suddenly the mighty tyrant slavery was judged by the righteous and true God. The sword of justice was unsheathed in righteousness against that which had drunk the blood of hundreds of bleeding victims. Angels might have pointed with admiration to him whom God made an instrument in liberating the poor slave, saying: "Behold a perfect man." The hearts of thousands are filled with undying veneration for the hero of liberty. His name will be ever dear to them who now live, and to generations yet unborn. The slave mother, in time of deep distress on account of the separation of herself and children, has devoutly prayed that God would raise up a Moses to lead them from the house of bondage to the Canaan of liberty. Thousands died without the sight, but not without the faith, for they had learned that sweet promise respecting their deliverance:—" Ethiopia shall soon stretch out her hands unto God."

Look at the present state of affairs: many, whose heads were raised up to the position of freemen, through the instrumentality of our Moses, now weep because he who was their deliverer is no more. We, who are here in Canada, the home of the free, feel the effects of the fall of the hero of liberty, and are here assembled to-day to show our respect for one who was foremost in securing to us the chart of liberty.

Dear friends, the tears which are shed so freely will not be forgotten; they will go up to heaven as a memorial of true regard for the martyr of liberty. We shall quit this part of the division with hearts responding " Behold, a perfect man."

II. THE END PORTRAID " is peace." The end of all perfection is peace. This is the paramount object of the death of Christ, to secure peace. This is the great end of the believer's expectation. the battle having been fought, the victory won, heaven obtained, and all their works crowned with the diadem of peace. When Christ was about to leave the world. on his triumphant march, he breathed this heaven born principle upon his diciples, "Peace I leave with you, my peace I give unto you."

Peace is in opposition to war. The desireableness of peace may at once be seen by considering the calamitous effects of war. The imagination has but to travel in the train of war and bloodshed to depict in living characters its terrible effects. Here a wounded soldier, beneath the tread of his comrades, suffering the most excruciating pain. There, at the sound of every discharged cannon, are many falling. mortally wounded. Look at the homes of the fallen, the news of the death of a son, a husband, having arrived, see the expression of deep grief by the wife, as she reads the missive containing the sad news of a husband slain. This grief is often increased, when the weeping wife looks upon her family of helpless children. Follow the same train of thought to the place where sits a weeping mother. She weeps because the news of the death of a son has arrived. Contrast this scene, with a country whose domains have not been darkened by the smoke of battle. Why are the inhabitants so happy? There is the wife and mother in whose eyes beam the radiance of happiness. There is no fear, lest the arriving post should bring the tidings of the death of a loved one, for the banner of peace floats in the breeze, and every heart rejoices in the sun light of true happiness.

There is another war, followed by another peace, which is the peace referred to in the text. The Christian is engaged in a warefare. His opponents are the world, the flesh, and the devil. Let us follow the Christain warrior to the conflict, see him unsheath his sword against the enemy of his soul, and march with quickened steps against the world. The world has been placed in the presence of the Christian in its most attractive garb, with the insinuating address of the arch find, " all these things will I give unto you if thou wilt worship me." Faith nerves the hand which holds the sword with strength, and bids him take a look through the telescope called faith, and see to the end of the present material world. Christian, what do you see? " I see the world, and the fashion of the world, yea all the haughty, and all that doeth wickedly in burning flames." Look again; what do you now see? " I see the old enemy also writhering amid the general burning." Thus by faith he overcomes. Through the same medium he looks beyond the present world, and sees with rapture mansions prepared for faithful warriors. Crowns of glory dazzle his dust-bedimmed eyes. Sweet music from the choir in glory awakens his heart to joys supreme. This is a foretaste of heaven—a shower of peace. The departed statesman had his conflicts ere he entered into his rest. His opponents, against whom he had to contend, were of three-fold nature. First, he had to contend with PREJUDICE. The first battle in this line began with his first election to the office of Chief Magistrate of the United States. It was successfully fought on the "Chicago Platform," the

principles by which he was ever afterward governed. The
enunciation of his non-extensive slavery principle so incensed the pro-slavery party, that they agreed among themselves to make war upon the champion of liberty, by
revolting against the government over which he presided.
The honorable chief called his constituents to sustain the
flag which they had called him to represent, nor did he call
in vain, for legions responded to their country's call.

Four years the contest waxed hotter and hotter; towards
the close of the second year a noble band of colored braves
offered their lives to be sacrificed, if necessary, upon the
altar of the country—I can't say THEIR country on account
of what followed their patriotic offer. They recieved a
reply to the effect that their services were not then needed.
Prejudice then assumed a more terrible shape than ever;
the hue and cry was raised on every side:—"THIS IS THE
WHITE MAN'S WAR." The President was doubtless grieved
at this insult to his friends, whom he was trying in every
way, to lift to the condition of freemen. Here the contest
with prejudice seemed to falter, the latter seemingly having
gained the victory. The godly Magistrate, being instructed,
doubtless by the Almighty, wrote the numerable emancipation proclamation, September 22nd, 1862, to go into effect
on the 1st of January, 1863, if the rebellious states would
not amply with the demands of the government. The
eventful new year's day came, frought with over four million new years gifts—gifts of liberty to the oppressed.
Who can tell the number of prayers of thanksgiving that
went up to God on that glorious day—the natal day of
millions. Heaven doubtless rung anew with the shouts of
its happy inhabitants! The banners of Christ shone with
new lustre! The Lord God had come "to preach good
tidings unto the meek, he hath come to bind up the broken-

hearted, to proclaim liberty to the captives and the opening of the prison to them that are bound; to proclaim the acceptable year of the Lord, and the day of vengeance of our God, to comfort all that mourn."

At length the monster prejudice was made to succumb. Our colored men were called into the raging conflict. Not one of them faltered, but they fought courageously for their bleeding country. God had seen the tears of his people, and come to deliver them, and to show that the power was in His hands. He made the sufferers instrument in effecting their own deliverance.

Success now crowned the union arms, and the terrible conflict was placed on the road to a successful issue. Again he was called to face opposition among his constituents, many of whom, not being able to see the ultimatum of the course he was pursuing, therefore they feared the consequence might prove detrimental to the enjoyment of the wished for peace. Lastly, he had to fight with the monster slavery. With one sharp stroke of the sword of justice, slavery was wounded to the death. Its grave was dug by " liberty," and covered so deeply by 'civil rights,' that it can never be resurrected until the judgement of the great day, when it shall be raised by the authority of the great Judge, to hear its final doom, and to be cast into the lake of fire with its father—the devil. The last enemy he had to meet was death, at the hands of a cowardly assassin. He is dead, but yet speaketh. His work is following him in a continuous procession, bearing aloft the banner of freedom, upon the folds of which is inscribed:—" Mark the perfect man and behold the upright, for the end of that man is peace."

> " Servant of God, well done,
> Rest from thy loved employ,

The battle fought, the victory won,
Enter the Masters joy."

" The voice at midnight came,
He started up to hear,
A mortal arrow pierced his frame,
He fell, but felt no fear.

" Tranquil amid alarms;
It found him on the field,
A veteran, slumbering on his arms,
Beneath his red-cross shield.

" The pains of death are past,
Labor and sorrow cease,
And life's warfare closed at last,
His soul is found in peace.

" Soldier of Christ, well done,
Praise be thy new employ,
And, while eternal ages run,
Rest in thy Saviour's joy."

Near the first of September I applied to the Rev. Dr.
Wickson, LL. D., for admission to the Toronto Grammar
School. I was kindly received by the rector, whose name I
have mentioned. On entering the junior division, I found
that the Grammar School was adapted to the wants of
all desiring to secure a liberal education, preparatory to
entering the university. I am happy to say, that, during
my stay (two years) in the Grammar School, my progress in the various branches was as good as I expected,
considering the amount of labor I had to perform in the
pastorate. At the sessional examination in December, I
was awarded a prize for proficiency in Latin. I began in
the first class, and continued until I reached the third class
in classics.

The memory of the Toronto Grammar School, with its
efficient corps of teachers, will ever be pleasant. It shall

be to me as one of the bright beacons, that has shone upon
my intellectual pathway with peculiar brightness. When
I think of its great end and aim my heart swells with
gratitude to God, who so beneficently bestowed upon the
inhabitants of Canada the great blessing of the key
of knowledge. I also bless God that these avenues of
learning are just as accessable to the black as to the
white man, provided he has the means to sustain him
self in the acquirement of that much desired boon—
learning. Had I the means I should stay here; but alas,
from the meagerness of my resources I am compelled to go
where I can do better. Trusting that God will aid me, I
shall start in search of an opportunity of gaining the great
desire of my heart—a thorough training in theology, that
best of siences. With a deep feeling of regret I shall soon
bid adieu to the Toronto Grammar School and the teachers
whom I greatly respect.

Nothing inspires my heart with a greater joy than to
live in a city noted for its many and elegant places of worship. Toronto is certainly the best gospel-fortified city I
ever saw. Having no service in our chapel in the evening.
I have an opportunity of attending divine service at any
church I may choose. I need scarely add, that, to attend
church forms my chief delight; I can sing, without the
least fear of violating the truth—

> "I love thy kingdom, Lord,
>   The house of thine abode,
> The church our blest Redeemer saved
>   With his own precious blood."

In passing the places of worship on my way to a parti-
cular church, my soul has been thrilled with great delight
as I would hear the deep peals of the organ, with the
melody of many voices, hymning high their Maker's praise.

I have thought if it be so delightful to be in the congregation of earthly worshippers, what will it be in the congregation of the redeemed millions, whose voices is as the
sound of many waters If it be so delightful to sit and
listen to the melting notes of the gospel from God's em-
bassadors, what will it be to sit in the presence of God the
Father, God the Son, and God the Holy Ghost, to listen
forever to the Son of God, telling of the wonders of his
cross. If the association of brethren be so pleasant and
agreeable, how shall we express the joy of our heart, when
we shall sit down with Abraham, Isaac, and Jacob, in the
kingdom of heaven. If earthly temples are so delightful
to the eye, rejoicing the heart, what will be the beauty
of the temple of the living God, which has no need of the
light of the sun, nor of the moon, nor of the stars, for the
glory of God is the light to lighten it, and the lamb is the
light thereof. O, may I be there, that sight to see, that
glory to share, where no sin shall ever enter, neither the
fear of the consequences of sin, for there shall be no more
death, neither crying, nor sorrow, neither shall there be
any more pain, for the former things are passed away.
What a blessed thought! What a glorious hope! I often
shed tears here, for this is a vale of tears, but the time is
not very far distant when I shall shed no more tears. God
will call me into mansions prepared by the voice of the
Archangel, and his mighty trump. I shall rise by virtue
of the resurrection of Christ, my Saviour, and then these
mortal tear-bedewed eyes shall weep no more, for God shall
wipe away all tears from my eyes. "Oh, for love like this
let rocks and hills their lasting silence break." Let every
thing that has breath praise God; let all the people praise
Him.

I have been called to witness death in the families of

friends, and in the family of which I am a member. I also know that death is sown in my mortal body, that it is desolving every day, under the influence of disease, but I look just beyond the narrow stream of death, and I read in characters divine, spoken by the mouth of God:— "There shall be no more death." I have a lasting comfort given me, even on this side the river—the victory of faith in Christ over the monster's sting. Christ has given me a sword made of the same material of that which he gave to all the saints who have fought with the monster death, and conquered when they fell. Let us follow one whom we shall notice in the combat; there he lies upon his bed—see him shiver, and ever and anon start as if suddenly pierced; he views instinctively the rapid approach of the king of terror, fledged with the instruments of death. He lays his unrelenting grasp upon the vitals of the struggling Christian. He awakes to the reality of the contest and finds that he is in mortal combat with the great destroyer. He feels that of himself he is not able to conquer, therefore he looks to Jesus, faith points to the sword which Christ gave to him. The dying saint with superhuman strength grasps his sword, and, with one sharp stroke, severs the sting of death. See his countenance beam with heavenly fervor; what is the matter now, hear him shout as he falls, "O, death, where is thy sting." He folds his arms in death, which has lost its sting, and swiftly speeds to glory, shouting as he flies, victory! victory! victory! through my Lord and Saviour Jesus Christ. See him enter heaven, and hear him shouting, glory! glory! glory! I am safe! safe! safe! I have fought the last fight! conquered the last enemy. Faith, hope, and sighing are exchanged for the fruition of heaven. Glory to God in the highest!

I hope to claim the sort of victory which I have just described. Sorrow is almost the constant companion of mortals here below. Many can take up the cry of the Psalmist:—"How long shall I take council in my soul, having sorrow in my heart daily." I can say that the cry of that man after God's own heart, has been the inhabitant of my soul at times. Sorrow is the opposite of joy. It may be illustrated in many ways. Suppose it is night, there is not a star to pale the sable canopy. A soul is lost in the dark, dense forest, his ears are saluted with the sound of wild and ferocious beasts. The owl sends forth his low, death-like moan; to deepen the gloom, a storm may gather, deepening clouds may start athwarth the skies, the deep-toned thunder may be heard, the forked lightning seems to split the clouds in twain, the rain begins to fall as though another flood were coming to drown the earth. A ship may be in a storm, the sails are riven by the howling tempest, the angry waves every moment threaten the terrified mariners with a watery grave; the cracking timbers are heard amid the wailing of the storm. The deafening peals of thunder appalls all hearts as if the judgment had come.

These are faint illustrations of what sorrow is. Sorrow may be divided into various classes. There is godly sorrow for sin; the sorrow of the world, which worketh death; the sorrow of in-dwelling sin; the sorrow of desertion; the sorrow of conflicts with satan; sorrow from wounds received in the house of our friends. Many of these are the heritage of Christians on earth. Many of these I have felt, which, like a dagger have pierced my heart; but I look forward to that period when sorrow shall be a thing quite unknown—"there shall be neither sorrow nor crying."

Pain is another evil to which flesh is heir. I have had my full portion of this part of the dowry of the human family. Often I have lain down to try to rest my weary, aching limbs, but no rest could I find. Pain, in its rapid flight, winged sleep from my eyes. The bone of my limb, which is necrosed, often pained me for hours, until sleep, nature's sweet restorer, forced itself upon my eye-lids, to the great relief of my body. I thank God that I can now rest both day and night, except it is when I have taken cold in the limb. It is sweet to look in God's book, and read the soothing sentence:—"Neither shall there be any more pain."

I started to write about churches and ministers to which I shall next direct my pen. There is the Bond Street Baptist Church, under the efficient pastoral care of the Rev. T. F. Caldicott, D. D. This edifice is one of the most beautifully finished buildings of the kind in the city. I have had much pleasure in attending this church, not only on account of its beautiful finish, good music, and large congregation, but because I could understand the word of God, as it was explained so lucidly and plainly as to bring the subject within the comprehension of all. I have often been made to rejoice with that deep and last ing joy, while listening to the story of the cross, the triumphs of the death of our Saviour, and the promise of his second coming. I was greatly impressed a few Sunday's ago, as the Doctor spoke concerning the day of judgment, of the joy that believers would then recieve, and of the unmitigated terror of the wicked.

I have visited the Richmond Street Wesleyan Church with much satisfaction. The Rev. Wm. Stephenson administers from the sacred desk, alternately with Rev. Mr. Pollard. The church is very spacious, the congregation very good. I have been transported to the highest of all that is sublime while listening to the words of Mr. Stephenson, who poured forth a profusion of eloquence like an ever flowing spring.

I have also visited the Elm Street Wesleyan Methodi t Church, and heard the Rev. Mr. Potts, whose mind is a store-house of rich treasures of the truth of God. The chapel is of fine finish, being furnished with a splendid organ, accompanied by a choir of unsurpassed excellence.

Knox Church, being one of the best Presbyterian Churches in the city, has an excellent congregation. I attended this church on the evening of the first Sunday in June. I was much pleased to hear Prof. Jones (a gentleman of color) lead in congregational singing.

The Evangelical Union Church, situated in Albert Street, under the pastorate of the Rev. Mr. Melville, is a church of the milder form of Presbyterianism. The pastor is a man of much ability. I heard him on the testimony to the Messiahship with great interest.

The Sayer Street B. M. E. Church (colored) is under the pastoral care of Rev. Peter R. Anderson. This church is well attended by both Methodist and Baptist brethren.

Last but not least is the Queen Street Baptist Church, over which I preside; it is certainly the best colored church in the city. It will seat comfortably four hundred people, was finished in 1841 by Elder Christian and others, many of whom are fallen asleep. I can say with pleasure that I never preached with more profit and pleasure in any church than in Queen Street Church. I have never been identified with a better set of brethren, all of whom seem to try to do the best they can to promote the cause of Christ. All the officers are men of ability, who occupy

their positions with honor to themselves and to the church.
I could particularize many private donations which I have
received from time to time, among them stand brother
James Johnson, whose donations I have largly shared, and
many others whose names I would gladly mention did space
permit. I have their names treasured in memory's book,
in which I shall continue to read them with pleasure till
it is sealed in death. There are many converts connected
with this church, whom God did by his Spirit call to re-
pentance under my administration. I can point to them
with pleasure and say, behold the monuments of God's
mercy.

LETTER FROM TORONTO, C. W.

MARCH 21st 1867.

Mr. Editor:—I hail with pleasure an opportunity to
write a descriptive letter of the times, in this part of the
Kingdom of Canada.

I must in the first place say something about how "The
People's Journal" is received here. Mr. A. Butler, a gentleman of color, has one of the most business-like news
depots in this city; and it is from him that the "Journal"
is obtained. I hope, Sir, that the "Journal" may meet
with a still wider circulation, both in Canada, and in the
United States. Geographically, we are, by many of the
people of the states, considered to be a little this side of
the North Pole, and consequently designate this part of
Canada, "The land of ice and snow." I disclaim every
thing of the sort, though at present the descending snow
flakes indicate that stern winter is very reluctant to give
way to "the time of the singing of birds." The past winter has been one of great interest to the people in Toronto.
It might perhaps be interesting to your readers, to hear

something about the institutions of learning, churches, etc. It is my privilege in common with others, to attend "the Toronto Grammar School," under the able rectorship of Rev. Arthur Wickson, LL. D. who is not only the principal of the school, but also teacher of Classics, Ancient History, and Antiquities. Of these springs of classic lore, we are daily invited to drink by our kind and honorable preceptor. Messrs. A. McMurchy and R. Scott are Mathematical and English Masters, both of whom are very excellent teachers. Several of the pupils attending the Grammar School are preparing for the University of Toronto.

The churches which I shall notice, are in a very prosperous state, some of which are enjoying continuous revivals. The Bond Street Baptist church, under the pastorate of Rev. T. F. Caldicott, D. D. is in the midst of a precious revival of religion, many have professed a hope in Christ, and scores are inquiring the way to be saved. I witnessed a very interesting baptismal scene, such as the church has often been favored with during the past three months, last Sunday evening. Five happy converts joyfully put on Christ by baptism. The Queen Street Baptist Church, the one over which I preside, is doing very well. The spirit of the Lord is often manifested in our solemn assemblies. Recently the sisters of the church gave a grand tea meeting on behalf of the church. Rev. Dr. Wickson and Principal Willis favored us with their presence; the former gave us a very thrilling speech, concerning the capabilities of colored men to learn any thing that any body else can learn. He also spoke of the position which the colored people now occupy as freedmen, exhorting us to diligence and perseverence, which, ere long, will secure for us the blessings of which we have so long been deprived Our Sabbath School is attended by both youth and adults; it is doing well. Mr. R. P. Thomas is the superintendent; his labors both as a teacher and superintendent are indifatigable.

The Richmond Street Colored Weslyan Church is in a very properous condition, judging from the attendance, which is very good. Mr. Wm. Abbott and others preach for that growing and interesting church.

The Sayer Street B. M. E. Church under the pastorate of Mr. Peter Anderson seems to be in a healthy spiritual condition. I was present last evening at a tea meeting for the benefit of the church. They will probably realize a very good sum of money from it.

Mr. Editor, I must close my letter for I fear I have already occupied too much space. In my next I will inform you of the ocular interests of the city.

Elder J. H. MAGEE.

TORONTO, C. W. April 8th, 1867.

DEAR BRETHREN:—I have to regard the mercy of God to me in bestowing blessings which have been the subject of my prayers for many years, viz., the restoration of my health, and the privilege of attending school.

After twelve long, weary years of suffering under the dark cloud of affliction, God has delivered me from suffering worse than death, under that terrible disease, necrosis, or death of the bone, which sapped the strength of twelve years of my life's morning. The providence of God, I believe, directed me to Toronto, one of the most healthy localities in Canada; and to a doctor whose skill, under God, has effectually eradicated the disease.

I have often prayed for an opportunity to study the Greek and Latin classics, and at length God in his mercy has placed me where I can enjoy the great privilege in the

8

Toronto Grammar School, under the able rectorship of Rev. Arthur Wickson, LL. D., teacher of classics, ancient history, and antiquities. Messrs. A. McMurchy and R. Scott are mathematical and English masters, both of whom are very excellent teachers. This is a preparatory school, in which students are taught the Greek and Latin classics, preparatory to entering the university at Toronto, one of the best institutions of learning on the American continent. It is my intention, if the Lord wills, to finish my studies at the university of Toronto.

The Queen Street Baptist Church, of which I have charge, is doing very well; the Lord often manifests the presence of the Spirit in our midst. There are two candidates waiting the ordinance of baptism. Peace and brotherly love attend us in all our efforts. We are as a unit, in trying to advance the cause of Christ. The Bond Street Baptist Church, under the pastorate of Rev. T. F. Caldicott, is enjoying a continuous revival of religion. I witnessed the baptism of five happy converts, into the fellowship of that church, a few Sundays ago. I learn that more are awaiting baptism. A new interest has just commenced in the north part of the city, viz., the Alexander Street Baptist Church. Thus the true banner is being unfurled in Canada as well as in the United States. May it continue to float upon the " flag staff" of the old ship of Zion, until she shall have carried the glad tidings to every land in every tongue.

J. H. MAGEE.

CHAPTER X.

THE OLD WORLD.

My Last Visit to My Home in Illinois—Toronto Grammar School
Theology—Thoughts of Faith About Spurgeon—Sword and
Trowel—Pastor's College—Trunk packed for London—Quebec
—Steamer Hibernian—Off for England—Passengers—Inci-
dents on the Voyage—First Sunday at Sea—Storms—White
Cliffs of Wales—Land Ahead--Landed in Liverpool--Thoughts
About England and English People--Curiosity of English Peo-
ple—A Colored Face—C. H. Spurgeon and My First Inter-
view--Mr. Spurgeon's College and Students--Rev. Mr. Brock
--In College -- Our Course of Study -- English Habits--The
Metropolitan Tabernacle--The Prince of Preachers--Sabbath
School--Catechumen Class--Mrs. Bartlett's Class--College Tea
Meeting--Mr. Spurgeon's Mode of Conducting Religious Ser-
vice--Contributions of the Congregation--An Outline of the
Lord's Work Done by the Pastor's College--President's Let-
ter--Rev. Newman Hall--Painful Sickness--Visited by Scores
of Kind Friends During My Sickness--Mr. Spurgeon's Birth-
day Anniversary.

My last visit at my home seemed to have been marked
with an unaccountable sadness—It was unaccountable at
that time, for it was then unknown to me, that, when I
returned again, it should be to see the last of my dear
mother. Every thing about home seemed to wear a look
of sadness, and at times my own feelings were oversha-
dowed by a sadness for which I could give no cause. I
remember the last breakfast I ate with my mother the
morning before I started to Canada. It seemed that every
bite of victuals would choke me. We hurried through the
morning meal, and my trunk was placed in the wagon, and
my father, and mother, and all the family went to see me
off. The cars are coming—I took leave of all my father's
family, but my leave-taking of all the rest of the family did
not affect me until I bid my mother "good-by." She

was overcome with emotion, and her tears flowed freely. The sight of those tears I shall never forget I can see her now as she stood on the plat-form of the railroad depot, watching the departing train.

That was a sad journey in the month of October, 1866. When I reached my home in Toronto, Canada, I immediately resumed my studies in the Toronto Grammer School. Having made considerable progress in some of the higher branches, I became exceedingly anxious to enter some theological school, where I might prepare myself more efficiently for the work which God had called me to do—that of preaching the gospel. When I first began to preach, I had an unsatisfying desire to see Spurgeon, the great London Baptist Minister. And I have often sat down at home with my dear mother, and read portions from Spurgeon's sermons, and said, "Mother, I do wish I could see and hear Mr. Spurgeon." My mother was always hopeful, and never discouraged her children in any thing that was right and commendable. She would say, "Henry, the Lord may open a way for you to go to England after a while." At length a pamphlet fell into my hands, published by C. H. Spurgeon of London, England, called the "Sword and Trowel."

From this little book I learned that Spurgeon was the president of an institution called the "Pastor's College," for training young preachers for the responsible work of more efficiently preaching the gospel. This set me all aglow with all my former hopes and prayers that I might be able to see Spurgeon, and sit at his feet and learn from him the way to preach in such a manner as to lead souls to Christ. I told my friend John C. Graves, who was then studying in one of the Toronto institutions of learning. I wrote to Mr. Spurgeon, and received a reply, that they then had more students and applications than they knew what to do with. In the meantime my friend Graves thought he would try the providence of God, and go across the great waters—like Abraham, trusting in God. He went, and succeeded in getting a place in the college. This gave me encouragement to go and do likewise. It was but a short work for me to make ready, for I was determined to go. I made known my wishes to the church, who very reluctantly gave their consent for me to go. The good sisters of the church looked after my wardrobe, and I was very soon ready with my trunk packed for London, England. On the 18th of May, 1867, I bought my ticket for Liverpool, England, via Montreal line of steamers. I embarked at Quebec in the noble steamer " Hibernian." Soon after I boarded the steamer, and arranged my " traps" and baggage, I heard the boom of a cannon. I inquired what that meant. The reply was: " That means we are off for England." Oh, how those words re-echoed through my mind —" off for England," how the memory of loved ones rushed across my mind, mother, father, brother, sister. The kind wishes of my church, and their " God bless you," was still ringing in my ears. " Off for England;" I thought of the wide waters of three thousand miles in length, ere I should see land, after we were out of the Gulf of St. Lawrence. The passengers on board were very friendly, and each one tried to be as agreeable as possible to while away the tedium of the journey. Our captain was a perfect gentleman and a Christian, always polite, always ready to add to the comfort and well-being of his passengers. Friday passed in silence almost, for all seemed more or less sad. Saturday came, and with it we found ourselves calmly settled down to the stern realities of a sea voyage. Sunday came, the day of rest, and with it the thoughts of our home, church, and people. By the kind permission of the captain, religious service was held, and at the sound of the ship's bell, which rung like a little wee church bell, in the same time, the strokes of the bell reminded me of the familiar Sabbath bell on land. It is near eleven o'clock, and the captain sends word to me, that the passengers are very desirous to hear me preach this morning. I sent the captain word that it would give me great pleasure to accommodate him and the passengers, but that for the present I must keep very quiet, for old Neptune had stirred up things so that it was not healthy for me to attempt to preach at that time, but that during the voyage I should be glad to preach Jesus to the passengers at any time.

In the evening the sea was calmer, and I felt better of sea-sickness, and on the broad deck of the ship, in the midst of the glories of a sunset at sea, I preached to the passengers from the text " With God there is no respector of persons." I took that text because I saw that some of the passengers were more anxious to hear "a black man," (as they called me) preach, than they were to be profited by what I might say.

During the voyage we encountred several very severe storms, one of which occurred at night. I shall never forget the terrific grandeur of that storm at sea in the midst of the shades of night. A storm at sea is grand above all powers of description. The vivid lightning! The rolling thunder! The waves howling in concert with the roaring of the elements above! At times, our ship was running on one side, while ever and anon a huge breaker would dash across the deck of the ship. Now we ride on a high rolling wave; now we are let down in the basin formed by two waves like mountains on either side of us. I tell you, dear reader, it may be very nice to read about a storm at sea, and wish yourself amid its awful grandeur, but I tell you there is no fun in being tossed about, first on your heels and then flat as a flounder. And when the bell rings for you to come to dinner, you sit down to a table fully furnished with all the nice things that a good appetite (under other circumstances) could wish, and just as you are getting ready for the dainty dishes, after you have eaten of the first course, you are suddenly called to run as fast as your feet can carry you, to the open air, and there divide your dinner with the fishes of the sea. Do you ask: "are you always sick while on sea?" I answer, that it is possible to get used to most any thing, and so a person at length gets used to the tossing and rolling of the ship, and then you may take your meals with some comfort.

At lenght we pass through fourteen days and nights, and the white cliffs of Wales make their appearance. You can well imagine the joy of all on board when the cry of "land a-head!" is heard. We finally landed at Liverpool, and then the work of debarkation soon took place, and in a short time we were snugly quartered at the Victoria Hotel, where we were all accommodated on perfect terms of equality. There was none of that foolish distinction shown on account of color that disgraces so many of our American hotels. I was treated the same as the other guests were treated. Every thing in England appeared beautifully strange to me, the landscape appeared in its most attractive garb. The beautiful hill sides dressed in living green, was a cheering sight after so many days and nights upon the misty deep. The day after landing at Liverpool, I took the North Western railroad for London, and in due time arrived at the Great Euston Station, in the great city of London.

Before I arrived at this metropolis of the world, my mind

was filled with some anxiety as to my safety and that of
my baggage, from thieves, etc. But when I alighted from
the train, all these terrible forbodings were dissipated by
the kind and courteous treatment of the officials, English
men, the true type of the gentleman. Instead of the din
and confusion, such as we sometimes hear from the clamor
of hackmen at some of our American railroad stations,
every thing was as quiet and orderly as could be. I called
a "Hansom cab," and was soon on my way to the place
where my friend J. C. Graves was boarding. As I passed
up and down the streets, I noted the great curiosity with
which the English people looked and wondered at me. The
little children seemed amazed, and some of them ran for
whole squares after the carriage, crying and shouting:—
"There goes a black man! there goes a black man!"
There certainly would not have been more amazed excite-
ment if a menagerie had been passing along the street.
The term "black man" is not used by English people out
of any disrespect on account of color. They use the term
as distinctive from white, the same as we say "a white
man," as distinctive from a colored man. It was very
cheering to me to meet a colored face in that beautifully
strange land. Having arrived at the boarding house of
my old friend and former school companion, Rev. J. C.
Graves, who was out at the time of my arrival, but who
came in soon after, we had a long and hearty shake-
hands, with mutual and generous congratulations at meeting each other after our long separation. This was on
Thursday afternoon in the first week in June.

On the next day I went in company with Mr. Graves to
the Metropolitan Tabernacle College, to have an interview
with Mr. Spurgeon respecting the object of my visit. At
the conclusion of Mr. Spurgeon's Friday afternoon lecture

to the students, on the "Qualifications of a Minister of
Christ," one of the students kindly introduced me to Mr.
Spurgeon, who greeted me in his usual kind and generous
way of speaking, and asked me if I was traveling in England. I told him the object of my visit to England was to
secure the means of a thorough education in theology, a
long cherished wish since my call to the work of the ministry. I was invited to remain to tea with the pastor and
students, in the dining-hall of the tabernacle. It will be
as well to mention just here, that every Friday evening
tea is provided for those students who live remotely from
the tabernacle, so that they may be present to hear the
lecture of Prof. Selway, who lectures every Friday evening
on some topic in the sciences. After due consideration
by Pastor C. H. Spurgeon and his estimable brother J. A.
Spurgeon, I was admitted as one of the students of the
"Pastor's College" of the Metropolitan Tabernacle Church,
London, England I found all the students of the college
most gentlemanly in their demeanor towards me, and
Christ-like in their life and conversation.

Having a letter of introduction to Rev. Mr. Brock, of
Bloomsbury chapel, "West End," I went the following day
to see him. I breakfasted with him and his family in
their beautiful home in the West End of London. Mr.
Brock is a venerable Christian gentleman, full of Christ
and Christian love and sympathy, so fatherly in his conversation that one is involuntarily constrained to love him,
for there is so much of Christ in all his conversation. He
encouraged me to remain in England and finish my education there, for be it remembered that it was not at first my
intention to remain there, as I went to England from
Toronto, Canada, to secure the means to enable me to take
a university course, under the superior advantages offered

9

in the university of Toronto, which would also allow me the chance of serving the Lord and my own people by preaching to them as often as my duties at college would allow. But God directed otherwise, and finding good advantages in the Pastor's College, London, and more favorable as to its course of study for my calling as a minister of Christ, I finally entered upon the course of study as before stated, in the Pastor's College, London, England.

The subjoined is a notice of my object in visiting England, from the July number of "The Freedman," published in London.

"DR. KIRK, in a recent speech at Boston, says of the colored people, 'the eagerness of this people to learn is one of the wonders of the age. Some said it was a spasm. If so it has lasted a good while. Their eagerness to learn is not dimished by difficulties, nor by familiarity with knowledge. We have never seen such eager scholars. The black man has developed splendidly. I exult in it.'

"We have proof of this desire for intellectual progress in the earnest applications made to us for aid to enable students of the colored race, who have the capacity to enter on the higher departments of learning, from which they are now prevented for want of pecuniary means. The Rev. J. H. MAGEE, of Toronto, has crossed the Atlantic on this educational mission. We have carefully examined his credentials, and find them to be eminently satisfactory. We commend him and his object to the few who are sufficiently interested in the progress of christian civilization, to afford to those who by their natural endowments are fitted to be leaders, all the culture and information that will tend to give the best direction to their course. Those who really estimate the importance of such a movement will well understand that the number prepared to sympathize and to help, must of necessity be few at a time when prejudice is strong."

The habits of English people with regard to eating are most astonishing to an uninitiated American. In this country we are satisfied with from two to three meals a day, but in England they eat from three to five meals a day; invariably four times every day is the general custom of eating in England. Breakfast about 8 o'clock, A. M., lunch at 10, dinner from 1 to 2 o'clock, P. M., tea at 5 o'clock, and supper at 10 o'clock. I was favored with four meals a day while I was a student in college. I usually breakfasted at 8 o'clock, A. M., dined at 1 o'clock, P. M., took tea at 5 o'clock, P. M., and supped at 10 o'clock. During one vacation I spent a week at a friend's house in Guildford, Surrey, and there we had five meals a day! I thought surely these good people will kill me with kindness; at least I felt solicitous lest I might become "foundered" by a superabundance of food for the inner-man. There is no use in saying "No, I have eaten plentifully," for the hospitality of the true Englishman is unbounded.

With regard to their church and chapel attendance as a people they have no superiors. As soon as the first church bells begin to toll the approaching hour of service, the streets are thronged with church and chapel goers. This to my mind was one of the most interesting features in English society—their profound veneration for the Sabbath and its privileges.

The Metropolitan Tabernacle is a massive stone building, with capacity for seating six thousand, and standing room for about one thousand, or probably a few less. There are two rows of galleries encircling the whole building, the interior of which is an oval, shaped like an egg.

This is beautifully lighted by numerous gas jets. This is the largest and most beautiful church edifice in the world. And what is more beautiful, this wonderful structure is filled twice every Lord's day with devout and interested worshipers, drawn thither by the most wonderful, as well as the most remarkable, preacher in the world. Mr. Spurgeon is certainly the " Prince " of preachers. Let me also remark that these crowded thousands are regular in their attendance every Sunday the year round, wet or dry, cold or hot, weather never diminishes the number of the surging multitudes who crowd the Metropolitan Tabernacle every Lord's day to hear the word of life preached by the world's greatest and best preacher. In connection with this church is a very large Sabbath school, numbering from eight hundred to one thousand scholars, whose young minds are trained every Lord's day from God's great book of discipline, which says, "Train up a child in the way it should go, and when he is old he will not depart from it."

There is also a large number of young men from various trades and pursuits in life, such as clerks, mechanics, and laborers, who are gathered into a " catechumen class," under Brothers Hanks and Bowker. These brethren teach the doctrines of grace as taught in the Bible, and illustrated by " Spurgeon's Catechism," a little book setting forth the doctrines of grace in a comprehensible and interesting manner. In addition to this there is a very large class of five hundred girls and young women, known as " Mrs. Bartlett's class." This devoted christian woman has been the means of leading hundreds to Christ. She is full of the Holy Ghost, and her whole life is one quiet christian course, reflecting the image and light of her Savior by her unobtrusive walk and conversation in life. Oh that the Lord would raise up hundreds of devoted women for the work of the Lord in America such as Mrs. Bartlett, of London, England.

It was my happy privilege to attend one of the great college tea meetings at the Tabernacle. Americans are unaccustomed to these social reunions, called "tea meetings" in England. They are conducted on this wise: A long table or tables encircle the lecture room of the Tabernacle, upon which are spread the whitest linen, set with plates, cups and saucers, bread and butter, and fine, rich fruit cake (the like of which I have seen only in England), and abundance of sandwiches. After the grace is sung by all in the house—

> " Be present at our table, Lord,
>   Be here and everywhere adored;
>   These mercies bless, and grant that we
>   May feast in Paradise with Thee."

These beautiful lines are sung to the tune of Old Hundred; and such singing! so even, round, and full, like the voice of many waters. Then tea is served, and while those at the table are eating, others in adjoining rooms are singing, singing the most charming hymns I ever heard. Oh, I tell you, these tea meetings are glorious times of social and religious reunions. They sing at their work; sing when on their annual reunions and excursions. The music of voices unites with the music of the rippling waters of the Thames as jolly-boats glide over its silvery waves. The result of this tea meeting netted £1385, making in United States money $6925. The result was swelled to this amount by pledges and contributions by persons present.

Mr. Spurgeon's mode of conducting religious service is peculiar to himself, that is, I have never seen any one conduct the services just as HE does; just a quarter before eleven o'clock the great preacher comes through a door leading from an upper room adjacent, in the rear of the tabernacle. He is followed by his Elders and Deacons, who seat themselves on each side of the preacher's stand (a small table upon which .ay a Bible and hymn-book.) Mr. Spurgeon walks slowly to the railing circling the platform, places his hands on top of the railing and says: "Let us pray." This is a short prayer occupying only a few minutes. He now gives out a hymn, reading it through, announcing the tune in a clear, soft, musical voice; the presenter or leader who stands to the left of the preacher, leads off in the singing. The preacher gives out a whole verse at the time, and sings with the congregation. After singing, he reads a chapter, or a part of a chapter, expounding verse after verse. After reading, he again engages in the second or long prayer, occupying from ten to fifteen minutes. He now reads another hymn, which is sung by the congregation without lining. After this, he takes his text and preaches forty-five minutes, very rarely exceeding or falling short of that time. Boxes are placed at convenient places in the great tabernacle to receive the voluntary contributions of the congregation. On a card, neatly and conspicuously arranged, is the date and amount of the previous Sunday's collection; this method is continued from week to week, so that every Sunday the congregation knows just what amount of money was taken up "last Sunday." Their Sabbath collection varies from forty to fifty pounds, in our money from two hundred to two hundred and fifty dollars. This is given away for the support of students attending the college, and is so stated in large letters on or over the contribution boxes, " weekly offerings for the Pastor's College." The pastor's salary is raised by rents from pew holders.

My college course was the ordinary branches of English, Arithmetic, Modern and Ancient History, Geography, Natural Science, Greek and Latin with an occasional lesson in Hebrew. Theology was made a specialty, Prof. Rodgers being our principal teacher in that department. We studied "Coles on Divine Sovereignty," "Charnocks works," "The Bible Hand Book," by Dr. Angus. Mr. Spurgeon usually lectured us once a week on "Matter and Manner of Preaching," and such subjects as "On adorning Ministerial Office," "The Authority of the Minister in the Church," "The Sabbath Question," "The Visitation of a Church," "Platform Speaking." These lectures were always interesting and full of meaning. Some of my most pleasant memories are associated with my interest in the Tabernacle College Lectures by Mr. C. H. Spurgeon. Mr. James Spurgeon took turns in giving these lectures during the temporary absence of Mr. C. H. Spurgeon from the city, or when he was otherwise engaged. I remember with very great profit one of Mr. Spurgeon's lectures on "Connection of a Sermon with the Text." Mr. Offerd lectured on "Types of the Holy Scriptures." Some attention was given to rhetoric. Lectures on "The Beautiful," by Prof. Rodgers; on the "Choice of a Text," by Rev. C. H. Spurgeon; "Spiritualizing a Text," by James Spurgeon; "Division of a Text," by James Spurgeon; "The Pastor's Oversight of Himself," by C. H. Spurgean; "Lectures on Logic," by Rev. G. Rodgers; "On pure extemporaneous Preaching," by C. H. Spurgeon; "On Exposition of the Chapter read," by C. H. Spurgeon; "On the Voice," by C. H. Spurgeon; also a lecture every Friday evening on some scientific subject, by Prof. Selway.

Quarterly examinations were had on all the subjects gone over the previous term, and certificates awarded according to the relative standing of each student in his class and studies.

OUTLINE OF THE LORD'S WORK BY THE PASTORS' COLLEGE DURING 1867.

PRESIDENT'S LETTER.

BELOVED FRIENDS:—You have my deepest gratitude for the help rendered to the Lord's work in my hands during another year. Although the number of donors is somewhat less than in previous years, yet the amount sent in is rather larger, and has been exactly sufficient to meet the expenditure, with only a few shillings to spare. Not a farthing has been expended upon collecting the amount, and thus your gifts, without deduction, have gone at once to the work in hand. We hope always to pursue this method, for we are sure that Christian willinghood ought to be sufficient to carry on the Lord's work without the employment of paid agents to scrape together unwilling doles.

As to our object in conducting the College, we rejoice that we have been successful in it beyond our own hopes. Our first aim has been to educate men of native talent, with good speaking powers, who believed themselves to be called to the work of the ministry. We persistently refuse men who are recommended to us as persons of character and studious habits, who, nevertheless, have not actually tried their powers of speech. We must have speakers; we can give a man education, but it would be useless to profess to bestow oratorical powers. We expect the men to have had two or three years' preaching at the least, and to have had evidences of usefulness following their labors, and then our object is to remove the rudeness of ignorance and supply the knowledge in which they are deficient.

Scholarship we do not despise or neglect, but our main
object is to educate the practical rather than the learned
man. We want, by God's help, in the first place to send
out good preachers, good pastors, good evangelists; and
secondarily, good scholars—good scholars, however, only
with the view of their being efficient preachers. We think
that God uses every variety of talent, but that the shrewd,
common-sense, rough-and-ready brother, when anointed
with holy zeal, be he learned or not, is usually the successful man: such men we seek for, and such men seek for us.
We have always scores of applicants waiting, and believe
we always shall have, for the institution grows in favor
with the young men of our churches.

Several gentlemen have applied to us both from the
United States, our Colonies, and Germany, and we seem
to be in such good repute, that when we have larger and
better rooms we shall, in all probability, be able to receive
a class of men, in good position in life, who will be able to
maintain themselves and become, from previous education,
preachers of a superior order. For this object we are
praying the Lord to send us a large sum to build suitable
class-rooms, more light and airy and healthy than our
present almost subterranean apartments.

Our course of study varies with the character of the
student; as will be seen in the tutors' notes, some men are
considerably advanced in Hebrew and Greek, and we could
wish that more were able to push their studies onward to
the higher points, but it would be folly, especially with
our short term, to attempt to drive all forward to the same
extent. The knowledge would be sorrowfully superficial,
and, for the sake of show, the more valuable departments
of study would be neglected. We attach great importance
to the Natural Sciences, which are taught by a gentleman

whose acquaintance with them is most extensive—who has, in fact, a passion for them. These yield a fund of illustration, and open up a field of thought compared with which classics (excellent in their own way) are but a barren mountain. A little anatomy, electricity, astronomy, or geology, while it affords relief from severer studies, is, at the same time, an enlarging of the range of the powers of the mind. To all we labor to give a liberal English education and sound Biblical instruction; failures there are, but in the main success has remarkably rewarded our efforts.

Our theology is Puritanic; neither hyper-Calvinistic nor Pelagian. We believe in the sovereignty of God and the responsibility of man; we hold predestination and free-agency; we see that salvation is altogether of grace, but we look for holiness as its result; we believe that the Holy Spirit works all good things in us, but we work out our own salvation with fear and trembling. We hope we have had a share in restoring to the pulpits of our country a clearer and fuller gospel testimony; as our sphere enlarges we hope to do more.

While with us as students, our brethren are exhorted to attempt to found new interests. Most of them during the summer are street-preachers, some of them all the year round proclaim the Savior in the highways. A service has been regularly conducted under the portico of the Tabernacle. In many cases a room has been hired in destitute neighborhoods, a small church has been gathered, a congregation collected, a larger room has been engaged, a chapel has been projected, a self-supporting church has been raised. Thus have many of our men made spheres for themselves. The fear of some old women of the male sex was, that we should overstock our denomination. Our answer is that we hope to increase it more and more. Since the College commenced, two hundred and fifty-three men have been received for training in its regular classes, and at lest four hundred and sixty have had instruction in the Evening Classes. One hundred and fifty-five students have gone from us to settle in the ministry, of whom one hundred and forty-four still remain in the work, the rest having either died, been laid aside by illness, or relinquished the work from other causes. Thirty-nine distinct new churches have been formed by the agency of our College. Twenty-two new chapels have been erected as the result of our agency. In London, at the present moment, we are making efforts to establish churches in eleven destitute districts. There are seventy-eight students in the College at this moment, and one hundred and seventy-four under tuition in the Evening Classes. Our men have, for the most part, either gone to old churches so impoverished as not to be able to support pastors, until they were revived and in many cases reformed, or else they have located in spots in which there was no Baptist church, and have built on entirely fresh ground. A notable instance is that of the county of Kent. In Bromley there was no Baptist interest till, by open air preaching, services in the assembly rooms, and other agencies, a church was formed and a good chapel erected. Sittingbourne—services in corn exchange, church formed, chapel built; Faversham—preaching in a hall, church formed, funds collecting; Sheerness—congregation gathered, church just formed; Whitstable—first efforts about to be made; Tunbridge—church formed, worshiping in town hall, minister settled. The County Association has been hand-in-hand with us, but it would not have been able to carry out these operations alone. We work with existing agencies as their fellow helper, and only wish we could find all our associations sufficiently spirited to encourage us. There is yet very much land to be possessed, and, by the aid of the Holy Spirit, all that is wanted is courage and determination.

It is encouraging to observe that our brethren for the most part remain at their first settlement, or have only moved where their sphere was too confined and a wider door presented itself. As a rule they have been very successful in winning souls, and the statistics of their churches are remarkably encouraging.

During the year we have published two works which are stereotyped, and the plates are the property of the College, Elisha Coles on Divine Sovereignty, at two shillings and sixpence; and John Bunyan's Water of Life, at one shilling. We hope by occasional publications to spread the truth and perhaps aid our funds. The grand volume of Thomas Watson's Body of Divinity we have ready for speedy issue.

We are strengthened in our conviction that our College is doing the Lord's work, and we earnestly ask those who think so to help us in our labors. We have no personal interest to serve in any form or degree, and therefore we ask boldly for Jesus' sake. We endeavor to expend the funds with the utmost economy, but, as in most cases we have to find our brethren with clothes and books, as well as board and lodging, our expenses will always be more per head than at institutions where all the students find a proportion of the cost personally or by their friends.

Before closing we are bound to thank our friends who contribute so constantly to the weekly offertory, which, as the account shows, is a large source of revenue. The Lord bless those helpers and all others, accepting their gifts for Jesus' sake.

C. H. SPURGEON, President.

VICE-PRESIDENT'S REPORT.

THE course of study this session as pursued under my direction is, with a few alternations, a continuance of that of preceding years. Each Monday and Friday afternoon all the students meet for class work, when lectures are given on homiletics, church government, Sunday-school work, missions, and subjects of practical importance to ministers. In the course of the year we have had the help of several brethren, in connection with these topics, including a deputation from the Young Men's Missionary Society, and our esteemed brother, Mr. Smith, the missionary from Africa; an exceedingly valuable set of lectures by Mr. Offord on the Types of Scripture; able papers by our brethren, C. Bailhache (on the Sabbath) and McCree on Misquoted passages of the Bible.

We are also indebted to Mr. Wigner for a lecture on the "Christian Ministry." Twice we have enjoyed an exposition of the principles and practices of the Society of Friends both in England and America, given by some of their most able men. Mr. Stokes has also delivered his lecture on "Memory," in the course of the session, and we have further had the pleasure of an account of the operations of the "Basle Mission and the Apostolic Highway," from the son of the esteemed brother who guides that movement.

With regard to class work, the students deliver in rotation a paper on Monday afternoon: the subject consists of a short essay on some part of English history, or the life of some noted statesman or king.

On Friday afternoon the books of the Bible, their authors, contents, etc., have furnished the theme of the papers which are criticised and supplemented by the tutor.

Church history, Roman history, Biblical history and the connection of the Old Testament with the New have continued to claim our attention, and the Greek history will now shortly come again under our notice.

I. The First Class has read the book of Joel in Hebrew, and is now engaged on the Psalms.

II. The Second Class has begun the book of Genesis, and continues the study of the grammars of the Hebrew and Greek languages, and has translated a part of the book of Acts.

III. The Third Class continues the study of " Charnock on the Attributes," and the Greek and Latin grammars.

IV. The Junior Class has completed the President's " Handbook of Theology," and has commenced Charnock, and the elements of the Latin and Greek languages.

I am glad to report that in my visits to the residences of the students, no charge affecting the moral character of any one of them has come under my notice. A few of the brethren have returned to their trade on the advice of the Presidents, but they do so carrying with them our warmest Christian love and esteem; and, though in our opinion not called to the work of the public ministry, we hope to hear of them as filling their posts in the church of the Lord.

Reviewing the whole of the year's work I am glad and cheered to be able to report most favorably. The brethren are walking in all unity of spirit and holiness of character, in the course of students' life, which will, I trust, in due time lead them to an honored and extremely useful career as workmen needing not be ashamed, rightly dividing the word of truth.

TUTORS' REPORT.

During the past twelve months the various classes have been well attended, and they hitherto have shown not only unabated, but increased ardor in study. Their attention has been directed to many and dissimilar subjects, and in all a distinct and real advance has been made. As some, though with considerable native talent, and with the true spirit for the work, entered the College suffering from a defective early education in English, special care has been taken first to remove this great hindrance to their usefulness by exercising them incessantly in the arts of composition and speaking, and then gradually to lead them to higher branches of study. Those who have come with a previous acquaintance of mathematics and classics have been taken through courses adapted to their different stages of proficiency; while all have attended lectures on theological, moral, and scientific subjects.

Mr. Rogers has been reading critical lectures on the books of Scripture; lectures on systematic divinity, conceived in a lively and interesting style, and free from the technicalities of the schools; and lectures on homiletics, moral philosophy, logic, and rhetoric. Mr. Rogers has likewise held classes for the study of the Greek Testament, Hebrew, and mathematics.

In Mr. Gracey's classes the junior students have been confined to the rudiments of Latin and Greek; the more advanced have read selections from Cornelius Nepos and Xenophon, and the seniors have been engaged in translating Cicero's De Senectute, the sixth book of Virgil's Æneid, the Clio of Herodotus, the first book of the Iliad, and the Acts of the Apostles. Arnold's Excersises have been used in both the latter classes as the basis of instruction in Latin and Greek composition. In the New Testament class, every endeavor has been made thoroughly to investigate the text and bring forth the most useful results of modern criticism, since a critical knowledge of the original is valuable beyond all price to the minister of the gospel.

Mr. Fergusson has kept the new men employed at the elements and higher departments of English, using chiefly Dr. Angus's Handbook as a text-book, and has taken large classes through a course of geography, physical and political.

Mr. Selway's weekly lectures on the physical sciences have been exceedingly attractive from their popular manner, and very instructive from the vast amount and variety of the information they contain.

It was my privilege to hear Rev. Newman Hall at the Tabernacle on America. This lecture was listened to by about eight thousand people. The lecture was most interesting to every one, and particularly so to me from my own knowledge of many scenes and incidents which he so graphically described. Mr. Hall is a profound thinker and an earnest and faithful minister of Christ. He has done great good in the cause of Christ, and exerted a wonderful power and influence in behalf of the bondmen in America. The memory of Newman Hall, like that of Abraham Lincoln, will forever be associated as the friend of the oppressed.

Towards the close of 1867 I was taken sick. My illness seemed to be a return of my old complaint, the affliction of my knee-joint. This was occasioned by a fall which I received while crossing the Atlantic ocean. It happened in this wise: The deck of the ship was wet and slippery from the washing of the spray and the swelling waves, which had been lashed into fury by a terrific storm which

lasted two days and two nights. Early one morning, after
the storm had somewhat abated, I attempted to cross from
one side of the deck to the other with a basin of water in
my hands; when I had reached about the middle of the
deck, by a sudden lurch of the ship, which plunged to one
side, I was instantly thrown with tremendous force on to the
deck; in falling my left knee first struck the deck, and
then my head. The basin of water went one way, my cane
another, and I was scattered about the deck in great confusion. I arose with a tingling sensation all over me and
a sharp pain in the bone of my left knee. This gradually
grew worse until it culminated in a serious swelling of the
knee-joint, accompanied with the most acute pain. I suffered so much from this that I had to retire from my studies: the pain being so great that I could not stand, sit, or
walk without suffering the most excruciating pain. My
knee became so badly afflicted that serious fears were entertained by my physician that an amputation of the whole
left leg, from the upper part of the femur, would be necessary in order to save my life.

It was just here that the critical moment of my life
seemed to tremble in the balance betwixt life and death;
now the trying time seemed to come. I could not walk; I
could not stand; I could not lie still, so great was the pain.
I was advised to try one of the best physicians in London,
whose services as lecturer on surgery had become famous
in King's College, London. By the goodness of God and
the careful treatment of my physician, Mr. Simon, I rallied
after a most trying and painful illness of four months,
during which time scores of kind friends visited me with
spiritual advice and prayers, among whom were Mr. Spurgeon and his dear, good brother James. Two and three
times a week from ten to fifteen and twenty-five would

10

visit me; some bringing nourishment of various kinds,
others all the little delicacies and fruits of the season.   On
several occasions I had enough confections at my bedside
to set up a small shop in a small way.   I shall never forget the kindness of those dear, good people, whose memory
will always be green, and associated with some of the happiest moments of my life.

Special prayer was made for my recovery on two occasions in Mr. Spurgeon's church.   God heard those prayers,
and in answer to them I was brought back from the borders
of the grave.

> " When all thy mercies, O my God,
>   My rising soul surveys;
> Transported with the view, I'm lost
>   In wonder, love, and praise.
>
> " Affliction's blast hath made me learn
>   To feel for others' woe,
> And humbly seek, with deep concern,
>   My own defects to know.
>
> " Then rage, ye storms! ye billows roar;
>   My heart defies your shock;
> Ye make me cling to God the more--
>   To God, my sheltering rock."

The following lines express my feelings when looking
at the goodness of God to me in all my past life :

> "My God, thy service well demands
>   The remnant of my days;
> Why was this fleeting breath renewed
>   But to renew thy praise.
>
> " Thine arms of everlasting love
>   Did this weak frame sustain
> When life was hovering o'er the grave,
>   And nature sunk with pain.

"Into thy hands, my Savior God,
   Did I my soul resign,
In firm dependence on that truth
   Which made salvation mine.

" Back from the borders of the grave,
   At thy command I came ;
Nor will I ask a speedier flight
   To my celestial home.

" Where thou appointest mine abode
   There would I choose to be ;
For in thy presence death is life,
   And earth is heaven with Thee."

After my recovery I was permitted to attend Mr. Spurgeon's birth-day festival, which was held on the beautiful grounds of the Stockwell Orphanage. It was on the 19th day of June, 1868. The air was sweetly perfumed with the breath of roses and other blooming flowers ; the trees were dressed in living green; the earth teemed with life and happiness. It was one of those dreamy days in leafy June when the very air seems agitated with the flutter of angels' wings. The subjoined is from my note book, penned the day after the reunion:

June 19th, 1868.—I attended the thirty-fourth birth anniversary of our dear pastor and president; saw the grandest sight I ever witnessed. First, Mr. Thomas Onley laid the foundation stone of the Sunday school house of the Stockwell Orphanage. Mrs. Spurgeon laid the first stone of the students' house of the Stockwell Orphanage. She was dressed in a light dove-colored silk dress. She wore a small bonnet (the fashion of the season), and white kid gloves. Mrs. Spurgeon having recovered her health from a serious illness of nearly six months' duration, was welcomed amongst the members by the young ladies of the officers of the church. A raised platform having been erected and covered with crimson, a number of the above-mentioned young misses assembled on the platform, upon which sat Mr. and Mrs. C. H. Spurgeon, Mr. J. A. Spurgeon, and many of the officers of the church. One of the little girls having presented Mrs. Spurgeon an appropriate written address and a purse of money, being followed by the rest who went up and welcomed dear Mrs. Spurgeon among them, each presenting a purse containing sovereigns.

The next thing in order was the tea, an abundance of which had been prepared. A table had been set under a commodious shed beautifully decorated with numerous scripture devices, such as "By grace are ye saved through faith;" "Let brotherly love continue."

I had just recovered from a severe illness of four months' duration, and was quite lame, but being provided with my "ponies," a crutch and walking cane, I managed to make my way near the table, to which my good brother, Rev. Mr. Ripper, brought me a chair, and sat me down in the midst of some ladies, who, by the by, were very happy to see me, and gave me such a welcome as made me feel very comfortable. One or two ladies waited on me by bringing the bread and butter and tea, which I ate and drank with great pleasure, talking the while about the beautiful day and the happiness of all around.

After tea a general rush ensued in making their way to the grand stand for the great open-air public meeting. Miss Walker carried a chair for me and one for herself. We sat down in a very comfortable place just at the side of the stand. On this occasion, according to previous arrangements, a presentation of purses to Mr. C. H. Spurgeon took place by the ladies, who had undertaken to collect money to present to him on his birthday. One after another of youth and beauty passed from the left of the

stand to the right, on which stood a large table by which
Mr. Spurgeon sat to receive the generous gifts of his dear
followers. The amount collected in one hundred and fifty
purses was £140, or the neat sum of $700. An additional
sum of a £100 was presented to him by Mr. Brown, on
behalf of the students of the Pastor's College, for the students' house; making, with a previous presentation of £300,
the round sum of $2700.

I must not forget to mention the band which enlivened
the scenic beauty by delightful music. Long after the sun
had set upon the thousands of happy hearts; when the
twilight of eve had set in—such beautiful twilight that you
might imagine it to be the return of the declining day—
the festive scene closed serene and bright, fitting emblem
of the illustrious birthday of one of the greatest and best
men that ever breathed the breath of life. May he live to
see many, many, very many happy returns of this auspicious day: and when the time comes for this eminent man
of God to be gathered to his Father in glory, may it be
the lot of the congregated thousands who have listened to
his voice on earth to meet him to pass an eternity of bliss
in the paradise of God.

I forgot to mention in the proper place the speakers of
the day, who were Mr. Spurgeon's father, Mr. J. A. Spurgeon, Mr. A. Brown, A. Mursell, Mr. Stott, and Mr. Brown;
Rev. C. H. Spurgeon giving the closing address.

Mr. Spurgeon's Tabernacle is one vast bee-hive of busy
christian workers. A daily morning prayer meeting is
held in the church from 6 to 7 o'clock. The Stockwell
Orphanage was built by the generosity of his congregation
and the assistance of friends at a distance. By the urgent
request of many of my friends who desired to hear me
preach, I rented a hall known as Carter street hall, where

I dispensed the gospel of Christ every Sunday evening for some time, to hundreds of interested hearers. I continued preaching in this hall until failing health laid me aside.

CHAPTER XI.

LONDON, THE METROPOLIS OF THE WORLD.

Public Buildings--Over Ground and under Ground Railroads-- The West End--Belgravia--Parks--Kew Gardens and Palace --The Goodness of God--Churches--The Bible the Secret of England's Greatness--"Ichabod," the Cause of a Nation's Weakness--City Government--The great Fire of London-- Tower of London--Crystal Palace--The British Museum-- King's Library--St. Paul's Cathedral--Westminster Abbey-- Hampton--A Letter from Elder De Baptiste--A Letter from my Mother--Preparations to return to America--Notes of kind Friends--Homeward bound--Home again--A sad message --Death of my Mother--My greatest Loss--Her Funeral--Both ready and willing to go--" My Way is clear and Heaven is my view "--Last Letter from Mother.

To form an idea of this great city, you may add the population of New York City, Boston, Philadelphia, St. Louis, Cincinnati, Chicago, Baltimore, and San Francisco together, and yet London, England, contains more inhabitants than all these eight cities combined! London is the most populous, as well as the most wealthy, city in the world. It contains more than three millions of inhabitants! It is situated in two counties, Middlesex and Surrey. The river Thames passes through the southern part of this magnificent city. In addition to London proper, the city comprises Lambeth, Finsbury, Kensington, Greenwich, Chelsea, and several other parts known to the people of England by their distinctive titles, but they all constitute what is universally known as the great city of London. It covers an area of about thirty-five thousand acres of land. It is nearly twenty-two miles in length and about sixteen miles in breadth; its circumference is not less than forty miles. The north and south portions of London are connected by bridges which span the river Thames. Some of the most notable of which are, London, Blackfriars, Waterloo, Westminister, Southwark, Wandsworth, Hammersmith, and several others of minor importance. The Thames Tunnel affords a passage way under the turbid waters of the river to those wishing to go under instead of over the river to different parts of the city.

"The London Docks cover about one hundred acres of ground, of which nearly a third part is water. The vaults beneath the warehouses have cellarage for sixty-five thousand pipes of wine, and one of the vaults has an area of seven acres." I wish they might use them for some other purpose than to store away wine to make people mad.

"The more noticable public buildings of the city are: the Tower of London; the Royal Mint; St. Paul's Cathedral; the General Postoffice; the Guild Hall; Mansion House; the hall of the various livery companies, or trade guilds; the Bank of England (covering eight acres); Royal Exchange; Stock Exchange; Corn Exchange; Coal Exchange; Custom House; East India House." The city is furnished with railroads both above and below the ground. Those above ground are constructed upon immense trestle work of brick, and it is wonderful to see the iron horse carrying his train over the tops of houses forty feet above ground. The train stops at various streets or stations, and passengers alight on to a platform and station house and descend to the street by means of stairways. The underground railroad is equally interesting and wonderful.

Passengers wishing to take the underground railroad have simply to enter a station and decend by means of stairs until they come within the enclosure known as the underground station. We have to wait here only a few minutes, and the scream of the whistle is heard, and soon the approaching train emerges from a sort of tunnel with its low, puffing chimney, blackened by accumulated smoke. The tunnel is kept pure by means of "air passes," and the cars are lighted by the tapers or lamps which are kept burning all the time. "Gower Station!" the guard shouts, and persons wishing to go out at "Gower Street," come out upon the lighted platform and go up stairs to the open street in the open light of day.

The most beautiful as well as the most fashionable part of London is know as the WEST-END. It is here that the rich and noble lords, ladies, and gentlemen reside. Their palatial residences are resplendent with all that wealth, art, and culture can make them.

The Houses of Parliament deserve special mention for their magnificence of architecture and beautiful finish. The upper house is called HOUSE OF LORDS, and the other is called HOUSE OF COMMONS, to attend to the business of the united realm of Great Britian and Ireland. Parliament was introduced by King John, as early as 1215.

A little way from the Houses of Parliament is situated Westminister Abbey, where there lay the bones of many of England's great men, and kings of the realm. Westminister is west of the river Thames, its limits contain the Royal Palace, at the extreme west of St. James' Park, and the fashionable district called Belgravia. This is certainly the handsomest part of London. Belgravia is situated around a beautiful circular park of blooming flowers, rare shrubs, and exotics, which are even beautiful in winter, but amid summer's milder skies, and gentle showers, it is lovely —a perfect paradise of lovliness.

A little north-west of Belgravia is Hyde Park. It was on a Saterday afternoon in October that I paid a visit to this celebrated park. It is impossible for me to describe it, such is the beauty of the rare plants, trees, fine walks, rolled as smooth and level as a floor, intersected by a body of water called the Serpentine. This was constructed by order of Queen Caroline about two hundred years ago. The park contains four hundred acres of land, and is now one of the most fashionable promonades of the weathy and nobility of London. The road-way around the park is crowded with carriages and horses, liveried servants, dressed in their knee breeches and white silk stockings, stand in pairs behind richly ornamented carriages. The driver and footman being seated in front. I was amazed at the powdered wigs, white as chalk, worn by liverymen and footmen. For over two hours the carriage drive, or road for carriages, was a grand moving panorama of wealth, grandeur, and beauty. It was here that I got a sight of some of the royal family.

Regents Park and Zoological Gardens are places of interest in London. Kew Gardens is situated about seven miles west of London. These magnificent gardens contain over two hundred acres of land; within these gardens is Kew Palace, a residence of English Lords and monarchs. These gardens are perfectly beautiful, certainly the most lovely spot of ground my eyes ever beheld. Walks laid out in great regularity, fringed with grasses of various shades of color, which surround blooming flowers of the most brilliant as well as the most delicate hue. I wish I could remember the names of some of the rare plants and flowers with which my eyes were so much delighted! When look

11

ing at the beautiful flowers, the green lawns, and stately
trees of these magnificent gardens, over which the clear
blue sky of a summer's day with a soft, balmy air, lent en-
chantment to the scene, I exclaimed :—" What a paradise
of loveliness! If it were not for sin, sorrow, and death, this
place would be heaven indeed!"   It is here that my mind
was wonderfully impressed with the goodness of God in
creation.   Surely this is a beautiful world in which the
Almighty furnished so many things which tell of their
great Creator.   My mind devoutly turns from these scenes
of fading glory to our Fathers house in heaven, where
things are eternal in their existence.   Here earth's fairest
flowers, and most beautiful scenes bloom to decay, but in
their short lived existence they seem to speak of the joys
that cannot die beyond the regions of this fading world;
there are glories which change not, neither is their period
marked by the flight of years.

London contains over four thousand churches and chapels, in whose consecrated walls the God of heaven and
earth is worshiped by thousands of devoted Christians.
Great Britain is the most wealthy as well as the most
powerful country in the whole world.   Her missionaries
have done more for the heathen, her money has printed
and distributed more Bibles than any other Chirtian country under heaven.   Now I want to remark to the inquiring
mind that the secret of England's greatness is found in
her love for the Bible, the Book of God.   The Bible is read,
and taught in their parish schools, it is read daily by their
families, it is taken into the work-shop and read at noon-
time, and whenever an opportunity is found.   The Bible is
found on most every ship, and certainly on every steamer
that plys beween England and the nations of the whole
earth.   Look at France. where the teachings of the Bible

have been discarded by most of its people. You have seen
the results—a loss of its temporal power, and certainly a
loss of its spiritual power. The wickedness of her people
is unparalleled in the historty of civilized nations. What
is the cause of her weakness! I emphatically answer: The
habitual neglect and disregard of the Bible! Let a nation put
aside the Bible for reason, or any other directing principle,
and "Ichabod" is already written on the frontlets of that
people or nation! He who would be great as well as good
must read and study the Bible! The nation that would
prosper, must build its foundation on the eternal principles
of the Bible, and make its laws according to the righteous
laws of God. The nation whose foundation is truth, has
" the eternal years of God."

The City of London is under a lord-mayor, aldermen and
common council. They form the richest city government
in the world. London is one of the oldest cities in the
world. Its history dates back as far as the invasion by
the Romans ; before this, however, nothing is known of its
history. As early as the reign of Nero, history tells that
it was an important city. It received its charter after the
Norman conquest, the original of which is preserved to
this day.

A monument now stands in the midst of the city to
mark the spot in commemoration of the great fire of London, which destroyed over $50,000,000 of property in the
year 1666.

The Tower of London is associated with the earliest
history of England. It occupies a space covering thirteen
acres of land, and was formerly used for a fort or fortress,
afterwards as a prison; now it is a storehouse for the armory ;
the crown jewels are also kept there. The main building is surrounded by two strong, high walls ; these are also

surrounded by a canal, which is usually dry, but which
may be flooded at a moment's notice. It was here that
Richard III. caused his nephews, Edward V. and Richard,
Duke of York, to be murdered in order to secure the throne
of England for himself.

St. Paul's Cathedral was built by Sir Christopher Wren.
This is one of the finest, if not the finest, public building
in London. Religious services are held in this house every
day by the English clergy of the Anglican church.

Crystal Palace is one of the world's wonders. Within
its ample enclosure is to be found on exhibition something of everything in the world of arts and sciences; also
many specimens of the animal and vegetable kingdoms.
It is also a grand bazar, in which many of the finest fabrics
are on sale and exhibition. In these collections may be
found everything in the notion line from a cambric needle
up to a sewing machine. This is one of the grand places
of resort for the teeming millions of Great Britain, for its
patronage is by no means confined to the people of London.

I listened with rapt attention to the singing of three
thousand children on one occasion in the great hall or
transept of Crystal Palace. It is impossible to describe
the effect which the blending of so many voices produces.
And then the great organ, which sets high up near the top
of the great amphitheater, is one of the largest organs in
the world. Its intonations sound deep, like the rumbling
of distant thunder. There are a great many departments
of great interest connected with Crystal Palace, the particulars of which I have not space enough to describe. I
would advise all tourists to pay a visit to the Palace before
leaving England.

Surrey Music Hall is famous for its having been first
devoted to the Muses. Afterwards its ample room and vast

ranges of seats were filled by thousands of persons on the Lord's day, drawn thither by the magnetic power of the gospel of Christ preached by Mr. C. H. Spurgeon. It is now used, I believe, for a hospital for the sick.

The British Museum is a famous place of amusement. It was founded by Sir Hans Sloane, a native of Ireland, but of Scottish descent. He collected a number of curiosities during his lifetime, and at his death made in his will provision to offer them to the British government for £20,000, which was about one-half of its real value. One among the many interesting things contained within the British Museum is the king's library, in addition to the national library. The gallery of antiquities, with the departments of natural history, book and manuscript. There are also within the same building mineralogical, ornithological, zoological, and botanical departments. The Museum is open to the public on Monday, Wednesday, and Friday of each week from 10 o'clock, A. M., to 4 P. M. The greatest number of visitors in one day was 42,000; the greatest number in one year was that of 1851, which reached the enormous number of 2,527,216. Multitudes flocked to the Crystal Palace to see the World's Fair that year, which accounts for the unprecedented number visiting the Museum. The apartment which contains the king's library is three hundred feet long and forty feet wide, with inlaid floors. Another very interesting feature is the reading room, surrounded on all four sides by galleries for the books, and lighted from the top. The British Museum is surmounted by a dome measuring over one hundred feet from the last floor to its top. The shelves are made partly of metal, and would make twenty-five miles in length. The principal librarian is the chief officer of the Museum. It is divided into eight departments, each of which is under a special officer called a keeper, with a number of assistants, whose business it is to go through their respective departments with visitors and explain the many things that are on exhibition. The library of the British Museum contains more than 600,000 volumes, and additions are made to its numbers every year.

There are a great many curiosities to be seen in the British Museum which I cannot attempt to speak of, such as animals and birds (stuffed) of every clime; grooved brain stone; music coral, coral reef from the Pacific ocean, beautiful coral, like tops of trees, from Singapore, India rope coral from Japan, coral in the form of a hand; and sea flowers; specimens of hand-writing of Hannah Moore, John Wesley (1787), Elizabeth Fry, Thomas Moore, James Gallary (1798), Edward Irving, Cæsar Borgia (1499), George Washington, William Pitt, Benjamin Franklin, and Martin Luther; note book of John Locke; book of prayers used by Lady Jane Gray on the scaffold, with notes in her hand-writing; book of prayers used by Queen Elizabeth, when a princess, in 1545; Hebrew roll of the Pentateuch written on African goat skins in the fourteenth century, etc. etc.

The National Picture Gallery contains paintings of great value by celebrated artists. Among the more noticeable paintings I jotted down in my note book were, "The Infant Christ," painted in 1505; landscape with Abraham and Isaac; "Embarkation of the Queen of Sheba," painted in 1600; "View of Venice;" "Dido building Carthage;" "Christ driving the money changers out of the temple;" "Marriage of Isaac and Rebecca;" and "Destruction of Sodom," with a great many other subjects of rare beauty and value.

The Indian Museum contains some of the most ancient

specimens of past ages, such as emblems of royalty, ancient tent cloth, Mohammedan temple, idol figures, " Marriage Procession of a native Rajah," and ancient musical instruments, etc.

Madam Tusaud's celebrated wax gallery contains life-size figures of all the celebrities of past ages and present time.

St. Paul's Cathedral stands on Ludgate hill. The first stone was laid by Sir Christopher Wren in 1675, and completed by him, after his own design, in 1710. Its height from the pavement to the top cross is 370 feet; its length from east to west is 510; width 250 feet; its circuit is 2292 feet. By an inside stair-way access is gained to a circular gallery within the dome, called "the whispering gallery;" from thence to the stone gallery, and further on to the golden gallery; from this position much of the surrounding city may be seen in clear weather. Above this gallery are the ball and cross. The ball is six feet in diameter, and is large enough to hold eight persons. The incumbent of this cathedral ranks next after archbishops, and enjoys an income of £10,000, or $50,000, a year.

Westminster Abbey. The first stone was laid by Henry III., in 1221. The larger portion of this ancient structure as it now stands was built by Henry III. It was completed some time about the year 1245. The length of the Abbey is 383 feet; the breadth is 203 feet; the height of the towers are 225 feet.

Henry the VII.'s Chapel is a magnificent specimen of the architecture of his time. It was commenced by him as a burial place for the royal family. Services are held daily, and on Sundays the service is well attended.

I visited the village of Hampton in June, 1868. Hampton is situated in Middlesex County, on the river Thames, about eleven miles W. S. W. of London. Its surroundings are very beautiful; its gardens and palace were once the most handsome, probably, of any place in England. Hampton Court was the favorite residence of many of the English sovereigns. This Court was originally built by Cardinal Wolsey for an abode of royalty, and every thing connected with the palace was of course made to correspond with the dignity and position of its royal occupants. The art gallery in Hampton Court contains a large and valuable collection of pictures, many of which are portraits of men who figured largely, and some of them notoriously, in English History. There are also a collection of pictures among them, representing some of the most important incidents in the New Testament. The following are some of the principal monarchs who made their residence at Hampton Court:—Henry VIII., Edward VI., James I., and his son Charles I., Cromwell, Queen Anna, and George II. The place is now open to the public free of charge. Many excursions from the great city of London during the summer months are made to Hampton.

Having received several very pressing requests for my service in America as soon as my studies were finished, I had already made up my mind to return to the fields of labor which were already white to harvest.

The following letters from Rev. R. De Baptiste were very cheering to me, as good news from home to one in foreign lands is always acceptable:

224 Fourth Avenue, CHICAGO Ill, U. S. A.

JANUARY 29th, 1868.

Rev. J. H. MAGEE:

DEAR BROTHER:—I have just received your kind letter of the 14th ult., through the kindness of brother W. W. Stewart, of Windsor. I also received the one you wrote to me some time before that one. Both of these letters gave much pleasure. I was more than glad to hear from you. Brother Graves, whom I had the pleasure of meeting at the annual meeting of the Wood River Association at Alton, in September last, informed me of your arrival in England, he having met you, he said, before his departure for home.

I am highly delighted to hear of your success in England, both in the pursuit of your studies, which I suppose to be the principal object of your visit and sojourn there, and also in that attending the proclamation of the gospel of our Lord Jesus Christ by you in that far off land. I do not suppose it will ever be my privilege to visit that country, therefore I take great pleasure in reading your descriptions of its people and customs, and especially of religious and educational matters.

A Mr. Huzzey, (if I do not forget the name) showed me a letter from you of introduction to myself. He has settled in our state. I met him at Elgin, whither I went to preach and administer the ordinance of baptism for a little church which I organized there about a year ago. I also met and made the acquaintance of two other genial Christian brethren from England who have settled in that town, the brothers Meirling, who, I think, came from Coventry. Our work over this side of the Atlantic is a gigantic one, and we have great need of zealous, self-denying Christions to enter upon and prosecute this work in the Spirit of their Master. My brother, I shall hail your return to your native land with joy. We need you now, we can spare you only to finish that course of necessary preparation which will doubtless add efficiency to your ministry.

We have very nearly completed our new house of worship; I think it a neat, pleasant, and substantial place of worship. We had the pleasure of shaking the hand of that popular English preacher, Rev. Newman Hall, in our house during his visit to the United States of America, and of hearing a discourse from his traveling companion, the Rev. Mr. Balgarner, also at our church.

We had a very pleasant meeting of the colored Baptists in convention at Nashville in August last. There was a large delegation present from the south, and many attended from all parts of the United States. Most of our ablest ministers were there, and all felt that our work was no unimportant one in connection with the evangelization and elevation of our long down-trodden and still oppressed and despised brethren—the freedmen of the south. I had the honor conferred on me of being chosen President of the convention for the year. We meet again on the Thursday before the third Lord's day in August, 1868, at Savanah, Georgia. I wish you could attend that meeting. Our corresponding secretary is the Rev. Rufus L. Perry, editor of "The National Monitor," Brooklyn, New York.

We have established several new churches in our state during the last year. Brother Graves is laboring with the church at Galesburgh, Illinois. Brother Wm. P. Brooks was installed pastor of the Chambers street Baptist Church, St. Louis, Missouri, a few Sabbaths ago. It was formerly the third church, but changing its location and name, it united with a mission church which had been established at the latter place, and obtained a good meeting house, and a large congregation thereby. It is now a very promising church. I have just learned of the death of old father Anderson; he died a few days ago, so I am informed. He has ceased from his labors, and is doubtless at rest in the "place prepared for (him)," for "there remains a rest for the people of God." What a work he has done in the vineyard of the Lord! And how well he has done it, considering his opportunities! Think you that you or I shall live to preach Christ till we are past our four score? Who would presume so much?

I would like to enjoy the privilege with you next Sabbath of sitting in the great tabernacle and hearing that wonderful man of whom I have heard and read so much—Chas. H. Spurgeon. Your many friends here send their kind regards to you.

Our city was visited with a most terrific and destructive fire last night. Our large wholesale dry goods houses and other wholesale dealers on the corner of Lake street, Wabash avenue, and Lake street and Michigan avenue, and through those blocks were destroyed to the amount of nearly three millions of dollars.

Let me hear from you again soon. My wife joins me in kind regards to you.

I am, very truly yours in Christ,
R. De Baptiste.

224 Fourth Avenue, Chicago, June 10, 1868.

My dear Brother Magee:

I received your letter of March 31st, mailed April 6th, in about fifteen days after date. I need not tell you that it gave me at the same time both pain and pleasure.

A pleasure it was to me to hear from you, and to know that you had been cared for by such warm hearted and manifestly Christian people. But I was pained to hear of your illness, and the suffering arising therefrom.

Under our Father's control afflictions have their profit, the hand that smites will defend, the power that wounds will bind up and heal. May you and I ever submit, knowing "it is the Lord, let him do what seemeth him good." I have received several favors from you, as the copy of the "Sword and Trowel," pamphlets, sermons, etc , for which

I thank you. I forwarded to you some papers containing an account of the dedication of our house of worship, also a letter in an envelope with one from brother Mukish. I am not aware that you received either the letter or the papers; if you did please let me know.

We had a very interesting meeting at the opening of our audience room. The opening sermon was preached by Rev. W. W. Everts, D. D., pastor of the First Baptist church of this city. The sermon was a good one, and produced an excellent effect.

I received a letter from brother Mukish a few days ago, in which he made inquiries about you, as to whether I had heard from you, etc. I hope you are again restored to health, and able to pursue your studies again. Brother W. W. Stewart is soon to leave Windsor for this state, which I hope will prove true as I heard it. We need his labors in this state. I wish you could attend the meeting of the consolidated convention at Savanah, which meets on Thursday before the third Lord's day in August.

Let me hear from you at your earliest convenience.

I am, very truly yours,

R. DE BAPTISTE.

In the latter part of May, 1868, I received a letter from my dear mother, the contents of which gave me great joy on account of my great love for her and my long absence from home. It seemed to me that I must go home, for my mind could not be at rest after hearing from my mother. Now I can well understand why it was that my mind was so much impressed to return home at once, for my mother was destined soon to quit this world.

SHIPMAN, ILL., April 21st, 1868.

MY DEAR SON HENRY:—I received your kind letter and was glad to hear from you, but sorry to hear of your affliction. I am in hopes that you will recover and be able to reach home once more. Put your trust in the Lord, He is able to take care of you. I am sorry you thought you were so greatly neglected. I would have written before this time, but the boys had written, and I thought they wrote what was necessary. Henry, if you will forgive me I will not neglect you so long again. I expect that you felt very badly during your sickness, thinking you were so far away from your people. I went daily with a sorrowful heart to think you were so far away that I could not be with you to assist you. I was in dread to hear again from you, fearing that you might have left this world. You must put your trust in the Lord; He is able to do all things.

I must tell you a little about my health. I have not felt so well for a long time as I have been for the last nine months. I have not lost a day's work the past winter. I gave Cyrus a very fine Christmas dinner; we missed you very much from the crowd. The protracted meeting at New Garden church resulted in great good to many. Leonard professed a hope in Christ. * * * *

Now, Henry, I must tell you something about my own self. I have been reclaimed and returned home to the house of the Lord. I was welcomed into the house of the Lord with great rejoicing. Henry, you do not know what a happy time it was when my children came and gave me the right hand of fellowship into the church. The joy was better felt than told. Henry, let not your heart be troubled; be ye of good cheer. I thank God I have gained the day. The Lord is on my side. He is my protector. *

Cyrus and Youreth hold family prayer night and morning. What a happy change we have had in our family. Henry, I hope, if in this world we meet no more, we will meet where there is no parting any more. Henry, I hope you will rest contented the rest of your days, and whenever you feel iow-spirited take this letter and read it. Henry, I hope you will rest satisfied, for I feel that I am on the right side of Christ, and will be the rest of my days. Henry, I have a great many good friends in Shipman for whom I thank God. Your second letter was read by a great many citizens of Shipman, besides many others, who said that if you ever returned home, that they wanted you to preach to them.

I hope, when we hear from you again, you will be better. I remain, you affection mother,   SUSAN MAGEE.

I read and re-read the above letter many times before I re-crossed the great waters. Every time that my thoughts were turned to the dear ones at home a sorrowful feeling would come over my mind, as though some one had told me that I would never see my mother again alive in this world. My forbodings were well founded.

I began to make earnest preparations to return to America; meanwhile making such additions to my library as I was sure that I could not make in America. Mr. Spurgeon, by the kindness of Mr. Blackshaw, gave me a fine collection of books of the Puritan period, viz: Sibb's Works, Goodwin's Works, Clarkson's Practical Works; and some of his own sermons. I regard this presentation as among the best collection of books I have made. Many were the prayers which followed me across the Atlantic from devout christian hearts The following notes are given as expressing the feelings of my many friends when I left England:

1 ALPHA COTTAGES, CAMBERWELL, July 16, 1868.

MY DEAR SIR:—I had greatly wished for the pleasure of a visit from you one day before you left England, but I am afraid I must now be disappointed as to this, as according to the arrangement of the office I am in I leave town on Saturday for my summer holiday, and shall not return until after you have left.

I am still more disappointed at being prevented, by an important business engagement, from seeing you this evening to say good bye, as I had hoped. I feel much indebted to you for your excellent portrait, and in return beg your acceptance of the enclosed photographs of my wife and myself, which were taken about the time when you first knew us. My wife will hand you this note; she joins heartily with me in regret at your leaving, as well as in best wishes for your pleasant and safe journey across the water, where we trust you may long be spared in the enjoyment of good health. I need hardly add that one line assuring us of your safe arrival would afford us much pleasure.

And now heartily wishing you God speed, believe me, my dear sir, very faithfully yours,

W. RUSSELL.

10 PENTON PLACE, NEWINGTON, July 22, 1868.

DEAR BROTHER MAGEE:—I am right glad of an opportunity of bearing my testimony to your consistent christian conduct during the time you have been with us at the Tabernacle. Your visits to the young men's catechumen class were always acceptable, and I am sure they would gladly join me in happy remembrance of you, and in wishing you a prosperous voyage home, a most happy reception by your own people, and years of usefulness in the cause of our Redeemer. That God may bless you, dear brother, and cause the light of his countenance to shine upon you and do you good; and that should we not meet again in

this life, that we may do so at the right hand of Him whom
we both love, the Lord Jesus, is the prayer of yours,

Affectionately,

W. BOWKER, Elder.

LONDON, July 20th, 1868.

DEAR SIR:—It is now more than a year since I made
your acquaintance, when you came to reside in England
for the purpose of pursuing your studies. I can now truly
say you have gained in my sincere esteem because of
your irreproachable conduct and many amiable qualities,
but above all other reasons for your love of the truth as it
is in Jesus Christ. which has lifted you above party preju-
dices. I have a good hope, therefore, you will continue to
make progress in further knowledge of God's purposes in
the church in these last ages, as He may be pleased to give
you opportunity to get instruction in the knowledge of His
will. Faithfully yours,

S. F. JOSEPH, Evangelist, Southwark.

METROPOLITAN TABERNACLE, NEWINGTON, July 13, 1868.

Mr. J. H. Magee has been for some time in our College,
and leaves us with the respect of both tutors and students.
His sickness cut short his time, as study was too much for
him while suffering so much! Otherwise, by his diligence,
he would have achieved a fair proficiency in education. I
commend him to the brethren among whom he may dwell.

C. H. SPURGEON,

President.

I have Mr. Spurgeon's letter as above, framed and hung
up in my study.

On the 23rd of July, 1868, I sailed from Liverpool on
board of the beautiful and commodious steamer Peruvian

The weather was very favorable during the entire voyage—the sea at times being as smooth as "a sea of glass," with scarcely a ripple upon the face of its quiet waters. In ten days from the time I left Liverpool I landed in Toronto, Canada, August 2nd, 1868, and found myself in my adopted home again. On Saturday, the 15th of August, about ten o'clock in the morning, a boy came to my boarding house with a dispatch. I broke the seal and read in breathless silence these solemn and painful words: "Come immediately, mother is at the point of death." Signed, A. S. Magee. I could not have felt worse at that moment if that dispatch had born a message to summons me away to the bar of God. I collected my things together as soon as possible and started home by the first train, but owing to the delay of the train, I had to lay by over the Sabbath in Detroit. That Sunday was a long and sorrowful day—the anxiety, the pressing errand on which I had started, all tended to weigh my spirit down under insufferable melancholy.

I arrived at home on Tuesday morning at nine o'clock, and found my brother in waiting at the depot; we went immediately to see our dying mother, who lived at a distance of two and one half miles from Shipman. She departed this life at eleven o'clock on the morning of my arrival. The saddest feature of this saddest of all afflictions was, that my dear mother was so far gone that she could not speak to me. Oh, if I could only have heard her pronounce my name just once, it would have been gratifying to my wounded and troubled heart to know that my dear mother had recognized her son in whom she so much delighted. She died in the full triumphs of a living faith. She told the family on Sunday that she would not be here when I come home. Her testimony was to the effect that she was

12

ready and willing to go. She said: " My way is clear, and
heaven is my view." "Oh, glory hallelujah." "I shall
soon be there." " I want you all to meet me in heaven."
She desired that I should assist Rev. W. W. Stewart in
preaching the funeral sermon, which took place the third
Lord's day in September, 1863. Elders John Livingstone
and Jesse Lee officiated at her burial on Thursday, the
20th of August. Her remains were interred in the Piasa
Baptist Church Cemetery, where they peacefully sleep
until the morning of general resurrection, when my mother
will awake at the sound of the FIRST trumpet. Elder
Stewart took for his text for her funeral sermon, "The last
enemy that shall be destroyed is death." 1. Cor. xv. 26.

I closed the services by transposing " Sister, thou wast
mild and lovely," to read—

" Mother, thou wast mild and lovely,
    Gentle as the summer's breeze,
Pleasant as the air of evening,
    When it floats among the trees.

" Peaceful be thy silent slumber,
    Peaceful in thy grave so low,
Thou no more wilt join our number,
    Thou no more our songs shalt know.

" Dearest mother, thou hast left us,
    Here they loss we deeply feel,
But 'tis God that hath bereft us,
    He can all our sorrows heal.

" Yet again we hope to meet thee,
    When the day of life is fled,
Then in heaven with joy to greet thee,
    Where no farewell tears are shed."

Yes, dearest mother, I hope to meet thee where we shall
recount the labors and triumphs of this life in the presence
of God the Redeemer and the holy angels. For a while I

will now say farewell, dearest mother, until the morning, then I shall look for you in the general assemble and church of the first born in heaven.

In the death of my mother I sustained my greatest loss in the world. There are few persons who can appreciate the real worth of a good mother. Let me say to all who are blessed with such a mother as I had, be sure that you esteem her far above every thing else of an earthly character. I think that there are few sons who love their mother as well as I loved mine. Most all my anxiety when absent from home was a deep concern for my dear mother. The following is the last letter that my mother wrote while in this world. I received it after her death, it having been forwarded to me from England to Toronto, Canada.

SHIPMAN, July 15h, 1868.

Elder J. H. MAGEE:

DEAR SON:—It is with much pleasure that I avail myself of this opportunity of penning you a few lines. This leaves us all in the enjoyment of good health, and I sincerely hope it may find you enjoying a like favor. Your very welcome letter of the 23rd ultimo, has been received, and its contents noted. We all were very happy to hear from you indeed. Especially so to hear that you are almost well. Oh! how thankful we should be to the Lord for his loving kindness to us. Henry, I do thank God that he has raised you again, as it seemed, from death's door. Henry, I hope that me shall meet again on earth; if we are not permitted to meet again here, I have a hope that we shall meet in heaven, where parting will be no more, and where sickness, pain, and death can never enter. I am happy to hear that you feel to put your trust in the Lord; he is able to comfort us in all of our distresses.   *   *   *

Henry, I feel thankful that you have so many friends. Oh! how thankful you ought to be for that great blessing! Have you any idea when you will be home? I would like very much to see you. You must come as soon as you can. You will please find my picture inclosed with this letter. Henry, I hope this letter may find you comparatively well. Keep in good spirits and get through with your studies as soon as you can, and come home. I think of no more at present to write.

I still remain your affectionate mother,

SUSAN MAGEE.

The above was probably the last letter that my mother wrote to any one previous to her death. How strange the coincidence of the date of this letter bearing good tidings, and the date a month hence, (the 15th of August) of a telegraph dispatch that my mother was at the point of death. Such is life. It is uncertain. Oh, may we all prepare for a home in heaven. To be with Christ is far better. I shall see my mother in that bright world of endless day. Jesus says: "I go to prepare a place for you. And if I go and prepare a place for you, I will come again, and receive you unto myself, that where I am there ye may be also!"

CHAPTER XII.

THE HAND OF THE LORD.

Professor in a Baptist College--Education--White Lights--Lincoln
--My Marriage--Removal to the West--Alton Colored Public
School--Baptist Church in Alton, Illinois--Called to the Union
Baptist Church of Cincinnati, Ohio--A Hearty Welcome--The
Lord's Work--Great Revival--Texts of my First Sermons in
Cincinnati — Inauguration Subject--Times of Refreshing--
Pastor's First Annual Report—What the Church Has Done--
Her Living History--Pastor's Second Annual Report--Great
Out-Pouring of the Holy Spirit—Testimonial—Union Baptist
Church Sunday School--Its History, etc.—Churches--Testi
monials--A Visit to Louisville, Ky.

In the month of October, 1868, through the kindness of
Mr. J. J. Cary, I received an invitation from Rev. N. G.
Merry, pastor of the First Baptist Church, Nashville, Ten-
nesee, to come immediately to take a position as Principal
of the Baptist College of Nashville; Rev. D. W. Phillips, an
estimable and cultivated gentlemen, being Principal of the
theological department for the training of young men for
the ministry. I went to this new field of labor as soon as
I could return to Canada and adjust my relations as pastor
of the Queen Street Baptist Church for such time as I might
be absent from them ; for I yet knew not how I might like
this new sphere of labor, but I thought I would go and see,
and perhaps make such arrangements as might be satisfactory to all concerned. I found the school in a prosperous condition, but suffering from the want of more teachers.
I went immediately to work in the midst of an increasing
attendance of pupils, until it was found necessary to open
a primary department for the accommodation of pupils less
advanced in their studies. Mrs. Fitzgerald was put at the
head of the primary department.

What our people most need is mental and moral training.

so that preachers and teachers may take positions as the
leaders among our own people. None can so effectually do
this as the people who understand their own needs, and can
sympathize with the deficiencies of their suffering brethren.
Therefore let us educate, educate, educate, until our people can take the helm and thus guide the ship of destiny
among our own people, until we shall have reached that
true eminence to which all true greatness tends—the moral
and intellectual development of true manhood and woman-
hood. Many have come to our assistance from the ranks
of our white brethren, for which I thank God. They are
yet laboring in self-sacrifice, and that of their own homes
and firesides, in order to help their colored brethren on the
road to the light of truth. We shall be the last to forget,
while memory holds its place, the noble deeds and heroic
devotion to the right when it was dangerous to be considered the friend of the black man. Such philanthropist
as Wendall Phillips, Wm. Lloyd Garrison, John Brown,
Owen Lovejoy, Henry Ward Beecher, Harriet Beecher Stowe
and a host of others, who have not bowed their knee to the
Baal of slavery, nor to its shadow—prejudice. I want to
add another name to the grand galaxy of liberty-loving
heroes and heroines, so that their lustre may shine yet
more resplendent with the light of liberty and justice. I
refer to Abraham Lincoln, whose deeds in the cause of
human freedom will live throughout all coming time.

Abraham Lincoln, president of the republic and com-
mander-in-chief of the armies of the union, proclaimed
freedom to all of our race within the limits of our country.
It was the grandest act of his grand administration. It
will send his name down "to the last syllable of recorded
time." He will be known in future ages as the Great
Emancipator, who gave freedom to four millions of mortal

beings. Borrowing the language of a distinguished American statesman with reference to George Washington, it may be fitly said of Abraham Lincoln: "The republic may perish; the wide arch of our ranged union may fall, star by star its glories may expire, stone after stone of its columns and its capitol may moulder and crumble, all other names that adorn its annals may be forgotten, but as long as human hearts shall feel and human tongues shall speak, those hearts shall enshrine the memory and those tongues shall proclaim the fame of" Abraham Lincoln!

On the 31st day of December, 1868, I was united in marriage with Miss Mary E. Armsby, of St. Louis, Missouri, by Rev. Wm. P. Brooks, pastor of Chambers Street Baptist Church of St. Louis, Missouri. I often now speak of my wife as being a New Year's Gift.

I continued to teach in the College at Nashville until the close of the school year in June, 1869, when my health failing, and my wife's health also being very poor in that section of country, I thought it best to remove out west to Alton, Illinois, where I obtained a situation as teacher of the Alton colored public school. In this capacity I gave the whole of my time for the first year.

In the month of March of the second year after my arrival in Alton, I was called to the pastorate of the Baptist Church of Alton, holding my position as teacher of the school and pastor of the church at one and the same time. With reference to my success as a teacher, the scores of children and youths who attended the school, will testify that their progress in their several studies was unprecedented. I made the reading of the Bible every morning a principal feature in opening the school, and then I would lead the children in prayer to almighty God, invoking his blessings and his guidance for the day. At the close of the school each day, all the scholars would repeat the Lord's prayer after me, standing, after which they were dismissed. As the result of this manner of managing the children by prayer, sixteen of those children were brought to Christ, and were baptized into the fellowship of the Baptist church. My work in the school was necessarilly very onerous, because I had all grades of pupils within the same room, from the A, B, C class, up to a class in Latin and physical geography, with intermediate studies.

THE COLORED SCHOOL.

ALTON, June 29. 1870.

EDITORS ALTON TELEGRAPH:

I wish to say a word about the colored school of Alton, and its teacher, Rev. J. H. Magee. As is customary at the close of the school year, all the scholars assembled last evening in the Baptist church to receive their prizes. The church was densely crowded with both children and parents, and, although it was extremely warm, the cheerful eyes and smiling faces of the children told that they cared not less for the heat, but more for the presents. When all were in and seated, their good and faithful teacher arose and gave a brief history of his labors, and told how fast the children had learned the past year, remarking that, although hard, his labors had never been more pleasant; that some of the scholars had learned exceedingly fast. Some, commencing with their letters, could now read, write, and cipher with great aptness. All the scholars received prizes of some value, according to merit. The prizes consisted of pictures, with and without frames; boxes of note paper; pencils, sceneries, albums and Bibles.

When all had secured prizes the teacher arose and stated that he had an additional prize, which he desired to give to the "best" girl in school. The gift was a beautiful little Morocco-bound Bible. And that the scholars might decide by vote who she should be. Accordingly they named two good girls, but the vote decided that one of them was better than the other, hence the precious book became her lawful property.

The prize question being ended, it was announced by the teacher that some one had prepared refreshments in the basement of the church, so that the parents could show how much they appreciated the good report of their children by treating them to all the good things, which would be pleasing to their taste as well as charming to their eyes. The evening being oppressively warm, each did his share in converting ice cream into sweet milk. Permit me to say right here, that of all the good—nay, very good teachers that our school has had, none have given better satisfaction to the parents or taken more pains to do justice to the children than Mr. Magee. Being amply qualified for the position, and having the children well disciplined, it is to be hoped that the School Board will appoint him the next school year, to instruct the youthful mind of our race in this city. And if there are many things which tend to make it a disagreeable task to teach our school, such as an ill-arranged and damp school room, we hope these things will not last, and that, ere long, the accommodations of our school room will at least be pleasant and agreeable.

G. A.

My father died in October, 1870, after a short illness, of pneumonia. He was a member of New Garden Baptist Church. My Father embraced christianity in the year 1851. He was a good man, as his life work, in maintaining a large family, after purchasing my mother and two children, well

13

attest. During his early life time he was enabled to accumulate much of this world's goods, but during the last ten years of his life he lost all of his landed property through the perfidy of a pretended friend. Let me warn all who have real estate to beware of "land grabbers," who may offer loans of money to you by securing a mortgage on your premises, only to secure himself for a limited time, but with the REAL PURPOSE of closing the mortgage at the expiration of the time given, and thus become sole possessor of the estate.

I found my work gradually wearing me away, but with no outlook for the better until some time in November, 1870, when I received an invitation to visit the Union Baptist Church of Cincinnati, Ohio.

CINCINNATI, OHIO, Nov. 29, 1870.

Rev. J. H. Magee.

DEAR BROTHER:—At the last regular business meeting of the Union Baptist Church, held November 25th, I was instructed to address you this letter, and extend to you, in behalf of the church, a cordial invitation to make us a visit and preach for us during your stay. The expenses of the trip will be borne by the church.

Hoping to receive a favorable reply from you at an early date.   Yours truly

JOHN H. CORBIN,
Church Clerk.

On Thursday, December 29th, 1870, I started for Cincinnati, to pay the Union Baptist Church a ministerial visit. Arriving at the Queen City on Friday morning at 6 o'clock, December 30th, I went to Mrs. Scott's boarding house on McCallister street, where I took breakfast. I sent word to

Elder R. W. Sott that I desired to see him. He came some time that morning, and directed me to Elder P. F. Fossett, on Race street, where I was kindly received by the family, brother and sister Fossett, who made me very comfortable indeed. Arrangements having been previously made by brother F. Lewis for me to stop with him, therefore brother Thomas Webb accompanied me to his house. He and sister Lewis made me welcome, and entertained me very comfortably. I found all the brethren and sisters very glad to see me, for they had been long praying that God would send them a minister, and they hailed my coming as the evident token of an answer to their many fervent prayers.

Saturday night following my arrival being watch-meeting, I was invited to be present and preach for them. The Lord helped me wonderfully to preach from this text: "O Lord, I have heard thy speech, and was afraid. O Lord revive thy work in the midst of the years, in the midst of the years make known; in wrath remember mercy." Habakkuk iii. 2. The next morning being New-Year's day, 1871, the members and congregation turned out very largely. I went quite early to the Sunday school, where I met and was introduced to Rev. Joseph Emery, the superintendent. I was very much pleased with the Sunday school, and the manner in which it was conducted. I was invited to address the school, which I did in the midst of marked attention by teachers and scholars. After the Sunday school was dismissed, I went up stairs into the main audience room, and took a seat near the stove. Soon after there came in an old gentleman, who came up to me and said, "How do you do, brother Magee?" He said he knew who I was, for he had been praying for the Lord to send them a minister, and that he had seen me in a vision or dream

before I came to the city. In his own words he said,
"Bless the Father! I knew him just as soon as I saw him,
and I said to myself, that is brother Magee, for he looks
just like the man I saw in my vision."

On Sunday morning at 11 o'clock, I preached from the
words of Jesus, John ix. 4: "I must work the works of
Him that sent me while it is day; the night cometh when
no man can work." The Lord wonderfully helped me in
the delivery of the sermon, and He owned and blessed the
word to the hearers. In the evening I preached about the
year of jubilee. Monday morning I returned to Alton,
Illinois. On the last Friday in January, the 27th, 1871,
the church extended an unanimous call for me to become
their pastor, which, after due and prayerful consideration,
I accepted, and entered upon the duties of the pastorate
on the 12th of February, 1871.

On the 19th of the same month I preached my inaugural
sermon from the text, "For I determined not to know anything among you save Jesus Christ, and him crucified."
2 Cor. ii. 2. The whole church and congregation, with
the community at large, gave me a hearty welcome in their
midst. God blessed our coming with the seal of his own
presence by an increased attendance upon all the services
of the church, which interest continues up to this day. I
can say with all fidelity that I have never found a better
set of brethren and sisters as a church in all my travels.
There is always enough of the living to bury the dead.
We held a meeting of some weeks which was greatly
blessed in the conversion of souls, and the encouragement
of believers.

At the close of my first year's duties, I had the pleasure
of presenting the following very gratifying account of
what had been accomplished during that time.

Pastor J. H. Magee's First Annual Report of the
Union Baptist Church.

Cincinnati, January 29, 1872.

My Dear Brethren, Sisters, and Friends:

It is my pleasant duty to present you with this my first
Annual Report of the work of the Lord in our midst during
the past year. The times of refreshing from the presence
of the Lord have dawned upon our church. There is a
great awakening among us, a mighty shaking among dry
bones. Everywhere are signs of aroused activity and
earnest zeal for God's glory and the salvation of sinners.
A spirit of prayer has come to us in answer to the inward
groans of His people. We tarried in faith and humble
dependence upon God until we were indued with power
from on high; and far beyond our most sanguine expecta-
tions we have been made the happy recipients of the divine
favor.

It has pleased the Lord, in answer to prayer agreeably
to his own promise, to bring many to accept Jesus, the
Savior of sinners. Among those who have professed a
good hope, through faith in Jesus, are several young men
and women who will be a power in this community in estab-
lishing a higher status of moral and christian greatness
among the youth of this city. The lamp of Christian faith
and love is burning brightly in every heart of our entire
membership. We feel to repeat the words of the psalmist,
"O clap your hands, all ye people; shout unto God with
the voice of triumph" God has given us a large and
increasing congregation to attend the preaching of the
word, which He has crowned with signal effect in the conversion of souls. During the past year thirty converts
followed our Lord in believer's baptism; received by letter

eight; under watch care nine; by relation three. There are awaiting the ordinance of baptism thirteen.

We have an efficient and well-ordered Sabbath school, in which God is blessing the word as it is taught from Sabbath to Sabbath. Rev. Joseph Emery is the faithful and earnest superintendent of the school, and has been for twenty-one years past. I bless God for giving us the labors of one so faithful and so full of good works. We have faithful men of God to help us as the standard bearers of the church, both in the deacon board and that of the trustees, all men of God whose entire sympathies and labors are with and for the church.

We have, in connection with the church, a Ladies' Church Aid Society, now one hundred strong, and it is only six months old. It is destined to do a great work for the cause of Christ and His kingdom. We have also a Church Visiting and Tract Committee, who are doing a good missionary work among that class of people who seldom attend any place of worship. The result has been a larger and more constant attendance at church. We are in the midst of a precious revival of religion, and are glad to say that general good-will prevails in behalf of the church and pastor.

Brother John Corbin is our efficient secretary—one that prides himself in doing his work well and cheerfully; for whose services, in behalf of the church, I write in heart felt commendation and thankfulness.

Brethren and sisters, accept the love of one whose heart's desire and prayer to God for Israel is, that they might be saved. Yours, in the love of Jesus,

J. H. MAGEE.

Officers of the Church.

Deacons.

STEPHEN IRVINE, JOHN LUCAS,
JACKSON MARTIN, WILLIAM KEALING,
L. H. HARROD, H. H. GRANDISON,
WILLIAM TALTON.

Trustees.

THOS. SKINNER, NATHANIEL NATHANS,
THOS. CLAY, R. G. BALL,
DANIEL KEATH.

Our church is always ready to give of her means to support the cause of Christ. They adopted the envelope system of contributing every Lord's day as the Lord has prospered them. I had the satisfaction of offering the plan, and the pleasure of seeing its practical bearing as developd by an increased amount contributed each Lord's day. The church owns a beautiful cemetery (all paid for) containing sixteen acres of land. This will in time afford a great revenue to the church.

The Union Baptist Church has always been foremost in every good work. During the dark days of slavery, the doors, hearts, and purses of her members were always open to aid the escaping fugitive on his or her way to the land of the free. As a missionary church, she has few equals and no superior. She is the mother of most of the colored Baptist churches in the State of Ohio. Some time ago, Elder Charles Satchell went out under the auspices of this church to New Orleans, Louisiana, and there planted a flourishing church, known as the First Free Mission Baptist Church of New Orleans. Just before his death he was permitted to see erected, mainly through his energy, a fine commodious brick church edifice, which stands as a monument to his energy and as a daughter of the Union Baptist Church of Cincinnati, Ohio. Besides the Free Mission Church, Elder Satchell organized a great many churches throughout the western part of Louisiana, which were gathered into an associate capacity numbering nearly twenty thousand members.

Below you will find notice of other churches recently formed as branches from the Union Baptist Church. It is impossible in the short space allotted in this volume to give a complete history of the work of the Lord which this church has accomplished since its organization. Her history is written in the hearts of thousands who yet live to bless the name of Jesus through her instrumentality. Many are gone to their eternal home to be with Christ which is far better, who hailed from the church militant worshiping in the Union Baptist Church.

SECOND ANNUAL REPORT OF PASTOR J. H. MAGEE.

DEAR BRETHREN AND SISTERS:

Through the abounding mercy of God, we are permitted to present our Second Annual Report of God's dealings with us as a church.

The past year has been one of great blessing to us as a church, both in temporalities and spiritual things. On the first of January, 1872, we began the year in waiting upon God for a blessing.

We continued in prayer amid some discouraging circumstances, until God came in convicting and converting power. We held meetings every evening except Saturday evening for nearly four months, during which time scores were added to the church such as shall be saved. Among them were many who had hitherto resisted every means of grace offered them, and who passed through many

times of refreshing from the presence of the Lord with
out receiving the blessing of pardon. During our meetings
the house was densely packed every evening, and the slain
of the Lord were many. We have received into church
membership during the past year one hundred and fifteen
souls, seventy-nine of whom were received by baptism.
'The Lord has done great things for us, whereof we are
glad.'' I feel like adopting the language of the Psalmist:
"Thou preparest a table before me in the presence of mine
enemies; thou anointest my head with oil; my cup run-
neth over. Surely goodness and mercy shall follow me all
the days of my life, and I will dwell in the house of the
Lord forever.'

God has given us a large and increasing congregation
of attentive hearers. We have an efficient and well
ordered Sabbath School, under the superintendency of Rev.
Joseph Emery, who has been twenty-two years in the good
work with our Sunday School. Brother Emery is a faithful, zealous worker in the cause of Christ. May he live
long to work for the Lord, and humanity amongst us.
The Ladies Church Aid Society has become an institution
of the church, and I trust that it may be as permanent as
the church itself. It is calculated to do good service as a
helper in the cause of Christ. We have a well organized
" Church Visiting and Tract Committee,'' who are doing
a good work in assisting the pastor and deacons in visiting
the sick, and distributing tracts among the people; the
result of this committee has been a larger and more constant attendance at church.

Our meeting house has been refitted and painted inside
and outside, from basement to audience room. We have
recently added another important stated meeting to our
church — that of a Church Bible School, which meets

once a week in the evening, for the purpose of reading the Scriptures, and hearing remarks on the same, closing with an essay by some one previously appointed to write on some of the doctrines of grace. These meetings are intensely interesting. Our church choir is among the best in the city, and is well supported by young ladies and gentlemen of the city. Mr. John H. Corbin is the efficient leader of our choir. Miss Elizabeth Corbin presides at the organ, morning and evening. She is very faithful in her attendance, and always prompt. Too much can not be said by way of commendation of the regularity and efficiency of each member of the choir. As they have contributed so much to the interest of the worship of God by their sweet melody here, God grant that they may sing His praise forever in heaven. Whatever has been done in the cause of Christ, we wish all the glory given to God the Father, God the Son, and God the Holy Ghost, sufficient for us is the " inheritance incorruptable and undefiled and that fadeth not away, reserved in heaven for us." It is our prayer that greater good may be done in the future than has been done in the past, that God may use us as instruments in his hands in bringing many souls to Jesus. Amen, and Amen.

J. H. MAGEE. Pastor.

THOS. MONROE, Secretary.

Present Officers of the Church.

Deacons.

Stephen Irvine,	John Lucas,
Jackson Martin,	William Kealing,
L. H. Harrod,	H. H. Grandison,
William Talton.	

Trustees.

" The Union Baptist Church was organized February 7th, 1835, with about forty members. Elder David Nickins was the first pastor, who continued in this relation until his death—a term of two years. During his pastorate, a great revival occurred, and one hundred and twenty were added. Elder Charles Satchell succeeded for a term of eight years, and three hundred and forty were added. Elder Allen Graham then took the pastorate, and held it, with success, for about eighteen months. Elder Thulkill followed brother Graham, continuing six months, when he died. In 1850, Elder W. P. Newman took the pastorate, and after holding it two years he went to Canada. Elder Henry Adams, who has recently died at Louisville, took the pastorate in 1852, and continued, with great success, until 1854. He was succeeded by Elder Charles Campbell for a short time, when he died. The next pastor was Elder H. L. Simpson, who labored very successfully for three years. Elder H. H. White was next called, and continued three years. Elder W. P. Newman was then recalled, and continued to the time of his death, which transpired in 1866. His success was very large. Elder H. L. Simpson was also recalled, and labored three years more. The church was then supplied by Elder D. W. Early for more than a year.

"At this point in her history, February 11th, 1871, the present pastor, Rev. J. H. Magee, was called to the pastorate. His labors have been abundant, and one hundred and seventy-three accessions have already been made. Present membership four hundred and ninety-five. The Sunday school, under the superintendence of brother Joseph Emery, is very prosperous, averaging one hundred members, and revival influences are enjoyed at the present time. Their place of worship was removed some years since from Baker street to the corner of Mound and Richmond, where they have an excellent property."

The Union Baptist Church and Congregation have been first in every benevolent work outside of her own immediate calls. The Colored Orphan Asylum has shared largely in her benevolence, as well as that of the Union Baptist Sunday School; the latter having made annual donations to the Asylum for many years. A grand union mass meeting, of all the colored churches in Cincinnati, met in Allen Temple on Sunday afternoon, May 18th, 1873, for the purpose of raising money to meet an out-standing debt of $1800 on the Orphanage. After brief addresses by Revs. Joseph Emery, Thomas Webb, and others, the pastors of churches called upon their respective congregations to come up and lay their offering on the table. The call was responded to with a will and readiness seldom seen in this or any other community. As is usual in such cases, the Union Baptist Church heads the list in her contributions. Many young people not connected with any church deserve honorable mention for their liberality on this occasion. Union Baptist Church and Congregation contributed $102.59; Allen Chapel, $74.80; Union

Chapel, $46.60; Harrison Street Church, $14.65; Plum Street Baptist Church, $4.00.

The work done by the different churches and congregations on this ever memorable occasion will never be forgotten. Its good effects will be seen during all coming time, "like bread cast upon the waters," it shall be found after many days.

The beneficence of our church is unbounded. They have shown their love and esteem to me in many tokens, which they have given in appreciation of my services as their pastor. May the Lord continue to bless them, is the prayer of him who loves to serve them for Jesus sake.

The Plum Street Church began its history as a mission, July 31st, 1867, composed of the minister and but one other man. It continued as such until November, 1871. The organization was then effected, consisting of thirty-six members, thirty-seven having been added.

From the outset to October 13th, 1872, there have been one hundred and forty-five accessions. The membership now numbers sixty-three, and the Sunday-school fifty. The church occupy a rented house that is adequate to their present wants, and they enjoy harmony and prosperity. Elder Thomas Webb has been their devoted pastor from their origin.

The Cumminsville Church of Cumminsville was organized August 21st, 1870, with eight members. The present pastor, Elder Peter F. Fossett, took charge of it September 25th, same year. It has had a net increase of forty-two, and now numbers forty-seven.

The church occupy a small rented room, but have purchased a lot and put in the basement of a house of worship

The pastor preaches three times on Lord's day. Prayer-

meetings twice a week, and a Sunday school at two o'clock
P. M., which was organized and carried on by the self-denying efforts of Mrs. M. L. Robinson, for many years before the church was organized. The school now numbers
forty-seven scholars and five teachers.

PRESENTATION ADRESS TO REV. J. H. MAGEE, PASTOR OF UNION BAPTIST CHURCH.

BY THOMAS J. MONROE.

MY DEAR BROTHER:

It affords me extreme gratification to be here on this
occasion, and to have the honor of being the representative
of the committee and your congregation.

For more than a year, Reverend Sir, have you been our
pastor, and during that time we have often had the opportunity to discover your merits, and to appreciate your
faithful labors in the cause of Christ. By your profound
logical reasoning you have persuaded many to become
good and true followers of our Lord and Saviour Jesus
Christ. In looking around us we can not fail to see the
intrinsic merit of your labor. To your untiring zeal and
ability are we much indebted for the prosperity of our
church. For more than a year have we enjoyed the bless
ings of your religious intructions.

> Thus far the Lord hath led you on,
>   Thus far his power prolongs your days;
> And every evening shall make known
>   Some fresh memorial of His grace.

We might stand here for hours and expatiate with rapture on this delightful theme, but words are inadequate to
express the deep feeling of gratitude we owe to you, as an
instrument in the hand of God. We invoke the gracious
assistance of our Heavenly Father that you may continue

to engage in and to discharge the very important duties imposed upon you, as to meet the divine approval of our Master, and secure the greatest good to the church. We trust that you will, in the future as in the past, prove by a cordial and judious ministering to us, that the sacred trust reposed in you is not misplaced.

But, sir, we will abstain from enlarging upon the many and eminent services you have rendered to us, and to the cause of Christ. Flattery were as unbecoming to ourselves as we know it to be distasteful to you, and we do not flatter. We can but thank you, and are ever poor in thanks. We have therefore taken the liberty of presenting you with this tangible proof of our graditute and acknowledgment. May you accept it from us as a token of our love and friendship, of our esteem for you as a gentleman, and of our appreciation of your services as a brother and a faithful pastor.

And now as you are our shepherd may you always emulate the example of the great Shepherd. Christ.

> See the kind shepherd Jesus stands.
>   And calls his sheep by name :
> He gathers the feeble in his arms,
>   And feeds each tender lamb.
>
> He leads them to the gentle streams
>   Where living water flows ;
> He guides them to the verdant fields
>   Where sweetest herbage grows.
>
> When wandering from the peaceful fold,
>   We leave the narrow way ;
> Our faithful Shepherd still is near,
>   To seek us when we stray.
>
> The weakest lamb amid the flock
>   Shall be its Shepherd's care ;

When folded in the Savior's arms,
We're safe from every snare.

And in conclusion, my brother, I would remind you of the parting words of our Divine Master: "Without Me ye can do nothing." And added to this the glad response of the beloved Apostle Paul: "I can do all things through Christ, which strengthened me."

Committee.

EDGAR WATSON,	THOMAS J. MONROE,
THOMAS SKINNER,	WILLIAM WATSON,
JOHN BENNETT,	JACOB ELDER,
GEORGE W. HAYS,	EUGENIE JOHNSON,
VIRGINIA BENTLEY,	SALLIE CRUETT,

MARTHA HAWKINS.

EDGAR WATSON, *Chairman.*
THOMAS J. MONROE, *Secretary.*

The Presentation was made on Thursday evening, May 16th, 1872. The present was an elegant dress suit.

PRESENTATION TO PASTOR J. H. MAGEE.

February 27th, 1873.

MY DEAR BROTHER:—Again I have this pleasant duty to perform—the honor of presenting to you another memento of love and appreciation. Permit me, sir, as a representative of Messrs. Nathaniel Nathans, Samuel Lewis, and others, to offer you this souvenir as an expression of our earnest appreciation of your services as a faithful pastor, and of our esteem for you as a gentleman, as a friend, and as a brother. We can but recognize such devotion in your arduous duties. We cannot too highly appreciate such high endowments, joined with so many personal, kindly traits: your frank, candid and joyous nature is such as to

endear you to all around you. We recognize in you one
that is ever ready to assist in the furtherance of any
scheme to build up the material, intellectual, and spiritual
welfare of the community in which you live. Let us hope
that in all your relations in life you may prove yourself
worthy of the esteem in which you are held. Accept this
slight token of love, not as a reward, for the reward we
are not able to give—it lies at the end of the race. We
refer you to the promise of our dear Master: "Be thou
faithful unto death, and I will give thee a crown of
life." And if you keep forever near unto His heart of
love,

> "He'll smile upon you here below,
> And give you the reward above."

To these remarks Pastor Magee made the following response:

Dear Sirs:—It is with deep gratitude that I acknowl-
edge your kind words, expressive of the sentiment of my
church and congregation. And to you, my dear church
and congregation, I tender you my sincere and heartfelt
thanks for this, another tangible expression of appreciation of my efforts to serve you, as your pastor. Accept
the reassurance of my constant and untiring endeavors in
the future, as in the past, to preach the simple yet glorious
Gospel of Christ in its purity and simplicity. It is my
aim at all times to try to edify, as well as to please, in
my public ministrations among you; and, above all, to set
forth Jesus Christ in such a manner as to lead the uncon-
verted into a saving relation to Him through faith in the
great atonement. Again accept the thanks of one whose
life is gladly spent in God's service with you.

The following letter from brother Corbin is here intro-
14

duced as exhibiting the kindly christian feeling that marks
the intercourse of pastor and congregation:

CINCINNATI, May 10, 1873

During the past two years there has been a steady increase of interest in the Union Baptist Church. The pastor, Elder J. H. Magee, has been active in every good work,
the members, in a good degree, partaking of his spirit, and
thus much good has been accomplished. When Elder
Magee came among us, the meetings of the church were
slimly attended, the younger members much scattered, and
many of the aged disheartened. The attendance now is
quite good at all the services of the church; the Sunday
evening meetings have been brought up to a good standard,
and the Bible school meeting supplies a long-felt want.
The church has indeed become a cheerful giver, and re-
sponds to every worthy call. The pastor is a ready speaker
and an active worker. His sermons are prepared with much
care and command marked attention. The church is enjoying a fair degree of prosperity. The members are gener-
ally united and in peace; and there are many cheering signs
of future growth. The dark hours of the past have disciplined many for the work still before us. God has committed
to our hands a great work; trusting in him may we never
falter—

" Nor lay Thine armor down,
   Till Thou hast won the crown."

JOHN H. CORBIN.

A brief sketch of the Union Baptist Sabbath School
during the past twenty-three years:

It was on a Sabbath morning in September, 1850, that an
aged brother of the Baker Street Church, Mr. Corbin,

visited the Ninth Street Babtist Church to secure some assistance for the school. The low condition and necessities of the Baker Street School were laid before Mr. G. F. Davis, then superintendent of the Ninth Street School. He looked over his teachers, and went to brother Joseph Emery, who was teaching a Bible class of young men, and said, "Now brother E., if you want to do some missionary work, go down to Baker Street Church, and help their Sunday school; they need help very badly, and you may do them good."

He consented to visit them, and did so on the following Sabbath. He found some thirty children and three teachers in a dark, dingy room. The result of this visit was that Mr. Emery bade farewell to his Bible class, to which he was strongly attached. New life was infused into the school; other teachers volunteered, and the school soon increased to one hundred, and went on prospering until two hundred scholars were gathered there for instruction. Rev. Henry Adams, about this time, became pastor of the church, and took special interest in the school. A monthly meeting in the afternoon, of parents, scholars, and teachers, was soon inaugurated, which was largely attended, and has been continued ever since.

After brother Emery had been superintending the school two years, the teachers and friends conceived the idea of presenting him a handsome family Bible. This was done in October, 1852, at the second annual meeting. The occasion was one of joyous interest, and will never be forgotten by those present. From year to year various other testimonials were presented by both scholars and teachers, which showed their appreciation of his labors.

The dark shadow of slavery, at this time and for years afterward, hung over the Southern States. The fervent prayers which went up to God from this church and Sunday school were in due time answered. No panting slave who sought shelter here was ever betrayed, but welcomed, fed, clothed, and assisted according to the divine word— "Deal thy bread to the hungry, and the poor that is cast out bring to thy house." These were the days which tried men's souls.

One Sabbath morning, Rev. Edward Mathews, an English Baptist minister, who had been preaching in Kentucky, came in, having escaped his persecutors. Nine times he had been thrown into a deep pond, in cold weather, because he declared "slavery was a sin against God, and a curse against man." He plead for his life, and was only spared because he promised to "leave Kentucky never to return." His touching narrative melted both scholars and teachers to tears. Many thanksgivings arose to God that the life of this faithful witness had been spared; and fervent were the prayers offered for the overthrow of slavery and the emancipation of the oppressed.

The superintendent, in those dark days, often assured the children of his conviction that they would live to see the end of this sum of all villianies; and he hoped to live himself to see the last slave emancipated.

In the summer of 1854, by excavations near the church building on Walnut street, the corner of the house fell down, and the Sunday school and church worshiped in the old Masonic Hall. These were trying times; but the band of faithful teachers toiled on, and in due time the house was rebuilt.

During the war, in 1861, the church found it needful to sell the old building on Baker street, and purchased the house now occupied, corner of Mound and Richmond.

Many a gracious revival has visited this church and

school. In 1857 scores were added to the church by baptism; among them many of the scholars. Elder Simpson was then pastor. Then in 1862, when Rev. Wm. P. Newman became pastor, there was a steady accession of members for some time—over one hundred. His useful labors were terminated by death from cholera August 1st, 1865: a loss severely felt by the school, the church, and the community. Discouraging and trying times followed.

Under the labors of its present pastor, Rev. J. H. Magee, everything has brightened up. He has taught a Bible class each Sabbath. May his life be long spared to win souls to Christ, and to build up the church in the faith of the gospel. Many scholars have been added to the church under his labors.

During the past twenty years the school has celebrated its annual reunion in an excursion to the woods beyond the city. These have been occasions of much interest and enjoyment. The profits arising from this source have mainly supported the school from year to year. A collection is taken each Sabbath for missionary purposes. During the past fifteen years the school has appropriated fifty dollars annually towards the support of Rev. Joseph Emery, city missionary. Donations to the Bible, Baptist Publication, and other societies, have been made; and special collections have been taken to aid schools and churches in the south. An annual donation has been made to the Colored Orphan Asylum.

Although several scholars have died during the twenty-three years, only TWO teachers and ONE officer have been removed by death.

The first was Julia Davis, teacher of a large Bible-class. She rested from her labors about the year 1854. Loved by her class and the school, she died in the Lord.

William F. Corbin, who was librarian for some time, died happy in the love of Christ in the nineteenth year of his age. One of the favorite hymns during his last sickness was,

> " Just as I am ! without one plea,
>   But that thy blood was shed for me,
> And that thou bidst me come to thee;
>   O, Lamb of God, I come! "

This was often repeated by him with great fervor. He was visited by superintendent and teachers many times.

Miss Caroline Breux, after teaching a Bible-class of girls for twenty-one years, fell asleep in Jesus April 4th, 1872. Her chief desire to recover was that she might lead souls to Christ. In this work God had greatly blessed her.

Many of the former scholars of our school are now filling useful stations in society, honoring God by a life devoted to his service. Some have become preachers of the gospel; among these we love to think of our brother Rev. Thomas Webb, who, after remaining with the school some twelve years, commenced the Plum Street Mission, which God has greatly blessed. The first superintendent of the Sabbath school, brother Joseph Corbin, was one of our scholars; the present superintendent, his brother John H. Corbin, has been and now is our vice superintendent. May God bless the labors of these brethren yet more and more.

Brother Joseph Corbin is superintendent of one of the best schools in Little Rock, Arkansas, and is State Superintendent of Public Instruction.

Another of our teachers, Samuel White, is superintendent of a Sabbath school in Alabama, and S. Sanderlin has a flourishing school in Mississippi. Herman Livingstone is doing a similar work in Mississippi. Some are in Louisiana and Texas. Rev. R. W. Scott, for many years a teacher, has charge of a growing church in Florence, Kentucky.

One of our scholars, Lizzie Warwick, married and went to Africa, where she died. Another married, and her husband, Mr. Turner, was appointed by President Grant an ambassador to Liberia. Others are in Kansas and Nebraska, and many others nearer home in Ohio, Indiana, and Kentucky. O, may God grant that all our scholars and teachers with their parents may meet in the Kingdom of God.

THE LATE WAR.

Every one of our members rejoiced in the election of Abraham Lincoln in 1860. Through the darkness which followed, and the terrible four years of war, we were enabled to see the hand of God, and recognized with the first shot fired at Fort Sumpter, the certain indication of the downfall and entire abolition of American slavery. In this struggle and its results was fulfilled that ancient prediction: "By terrible things in righteousness wilt thou answer us, O God of our salvation."

Many of our scholars were enlisted in the army, and all felt a deep interest in the struggle. All the male teachers and the superintendent went to the rescue, when our city was threatened in 1862. Busy hands were employed, and many offerings made to our suffering soldiers.

Our brethren from the south were sent to our city by the hundreds, and our school did its part in helping these poor, distressed people. Some of them remain among us, and are industrious, pious men and women. They were welcomed into the school and the church of Christ.

In the assassination of our lamented President, Abraham Lincoln, our school sympathized with the nation in its heartfelt sorrow, ever keeping the country and its rulers in their hearts before God in prayer.

Brighter days have dawned under our much esteemed President Grant. May God bless him, and spare his life for many years.

Our School has been visited by men of God from the east and west, north and south. Cleveland, Boston, New York, Washington, St. Louis, Chicago, and New Orleans have been represented by earnest Christian workers, whose words have cheered our hearts.

Brethren of our city have always shown a readiness to visit us. Brother H. T. Miller, and our brother W. H. Doane, author of "Silver Spray," have many times gladdened our hearts by earnest words of Christian love.

PRESENT OFFICERS OF THE SCHOOL.

Superintendent—JOSEPH EMERY.

Vice-Superintendent—JOHN H. CORBIN.

Secretary—MARY FORTE.

Treasurer—GEORGE HARRISON.

Librarians.

GRIFFITH FORTE,   HENRY BAKER.

Teachers.

REV. J. H. MAGEE,	MRS. ISABELLA GRAHAM,
G. W. FORBES,	MRS. ADELIA CURTIS,
FOUNTAIN LEWIS,	MRS. J. H. CORBIN.
J. H. CORBIN,	MISS ELLA COLLINS,
GEO. HAYS,	MISS MARY LEWIS,
GEO. HARRISON,	MISS ADA SHORT,
MRS. FANNIE MONROE,	MISS JULIA SHORT (deceased)

Whatever of good the school has accomplished, its teachers and officers desire to say, "Not unto us, O Lord, not unto us, but to thy name give glory." "Of thine own have we given unto thee." Whilst praising God for the many blessings bestowed upon us, we mourn our short-comings, and earnestly pray that our lives may be more entirely consecrated to Christ, that all the children com-mitted to our care may become the children of God by faith in Jesus Christ, that their lives may be devoted to His service. And when it shall please God to remove us, that we may depart and be with Christ, which is far better.

Cincinnati, May 1st. 1873.

Allen Temple, formerly known as Allen Chapel, is a beautiful structure known as the Jewish Synagogue, situ-ated on corner of Broadway and Sixth. It is a noteworthy fact that this is the first instance of a Jewish place of worship having passed into the hands of colored people. The surroundings of their old church were any thing else than agreeable. In process of time their present beautiful house, more beautiful in architecture, and also more beau-tiful for its situation, was offered by the Jews for sale. Many applications were made for it, but the former owners preferred that the house should pass into the hands of a denomination who would use its sacred inclosure for the worship of the true God. Through the untiring energy of their faithful pastor, Rev. R. A. Johnson, and the saga-city of his church officers, the purchase was made at a cost of \$25 000, and dedicated to the worship of almighty God on the 4th of December, 1870, by the A M. E. Church. The sermon was preached by Rev. Bishop D. A. Payne, D. D. Now they have one of the finest, if not the finest, church edifice in the western country. It will seat about one thousand people.

Now a few words about the present pastor Rev. R. A.

15

Johnson, who has been preaching the gospel for twenty years. He is one of the most vigorous, polished, and ready speakers in the A. M. E. Church. Under God his labors have been, and are yet abundantly blessed. As a financier he has no superior. Through this ability in this matter the A. M. E. Church and denomination owe a lasting debt of gratitude for what he has accomplished. Our personal and social relations during his stay in Cincinnati were most pleasant and agreeable, he and I frequently exchanging pulpits to the mutal satisfaction of our respective charges. It is with deep regret that our pleasant relations as co-workers in the cause of our Lord and Saviour is soon to be severed by his call and settlement with another charge. Though we may be each laboring in separate and it may be distant fields of usefulness, yet the memories of happy by-gone days shall cluster around our pathways in this life like Jonathan and David, who lived and died as one

" Blest be the tie that binds
Our hearts in Christian love ;
The fellowship of kindred minds
Is like to that above.

" When we asunder part
It gives us inward pain,
But we shall still be joined in heart.
And hope to meet again."

Walnut Hills Baptist Church was organized under their present successful pastor, Elder D. W. Early. The church has had a steady growth since its organization, and, judging from its past history, it is destined to be one of the strongest churches in southern Ohio.

First Baptist Church of Florence, Kentucky, was organized on the 10th of August, 1870, under a large beech tree about one mile above Florence. Elder R. W. Scott was called to preach for the people, and seeing such numbers, like one of old, he inquired, "Who is on the Lord's side." Out of the multitude he found four persons who dared to say that they were on the Lord's side. With them Elder Scott made a covenant to become an organized body. At that time they had no house in which to worship God, but since that time, by the help of the Lord, they have purchased a large lot, and built a comfortable house capable of accommodating three hundred persons. They have a flourishing Sunday school, and a congregation of over two hundred people. "The wilderness and the solitary place shall be glad for them; and the desert shall blossom as a rose." Isaiah xxxv. 1.

Union M. E. Church (pastor, Elder Swere) is doing very well under their present pastor. They have enjoyed a precious revival of religion since brother Swere took the pastoral oversight of them. Their present beautiful house of worship, on Seventh street, is very comfortable. Signs of progress are very evident in their growing congregation.

Harrison Street Christian Church, under the pastoral charge of Rev. Rufus Conrad, is doing a good work for God. Pastor Elder Conrad is a studious and profound thinker—a man calculated to do much good. His services are in great demand both in Cincinnati and elsewhere.

Zion Baptist Church was organized many years ago, and through their ex-pastor Elder Wallace Shelton, they gained a wonderful degree of prominence. They succeeded in building their present large and beautiful house of worship on Ninth Street, where they have an excellent prop-

erty, and it is to be hoped that they may soon be relieved
from a heavy **debt** which now embarrasses them. Their
house is on**e** of **the** finest structures among the colored
Baptists in the west.

Elder Shelton's labors as a planter of churches have
been abundant. As he is about to write a history of his
life and work in the State of Ohio, I here only give a
brief notice of his connection, as pastor, with the Zion
Baptist Church, which relation has been severed by his
resignation. For further particulars I take great pleasure
in referring the reader to Elder Shelton's forth coming
book.

A TRIP TO LOUISVILLE, KENTUCKY.

On Saturday, April 26th, 1873, I went to Louisville, via
the Short Line Railroad, arriving about 1 o'clock in the
afternoon of the day of my departure. I stopped at the
residence of Mr. Austin Hubbard, on Ninth street, by
whom I was introduced to Elder Andrew Heth, pastor of
Fifth Street Baptist Church (late Elder Adams' church).
I found Elder Heth a very genial, Christ loving, christian
brother, and received from him and his church people a
very hearty welcome. I visited their Sunday school, which
I found to be well organized and under an efficient number
of teachers. Their superintendent is a very excellent
young man, who is doing a good work for that school and
for the church of Christ. There were three hundred and
thirteen scholars present on the morning of the 27th of
April. The superintendent asked me to address the school
at the close of class exercises, which I did, taking for my
subject the importance of early religious training, illustrated by the spring season of the year.

In the evening, at 8 o'clock, I preached to a crowded congregation of attentive hearers. This is one of the largest churches (numerically) in the south-western country. This church, without any exception, has one of the best choirs in the United States. Mr. Minnis is the leader of this very excellent choir.

At 3 o'clock, P. M., I preached in the York Street Baptist Church, corner of Fifth and York streets. Elder W. W. Taylor is the pastor of this thriving new church. He has labored abundantly with his willing flock in getting means with which to build the present new and commodious house of worship. The building is made of brick, and when completed it will be one of the most beautiful houses of worship among the colored Baptists in that city. There are eight colored Baptist churches in Louisville— the Fifth, York, and Green Street churches being the principal ones. Elder Gaddy is the pastor of the last named.

My visit to Louisville was attended with feelings of emotion in consequence of its association with the early history of my father and mother. It was in that city that my mother was born, and my father was born very near the city, near Bear Grass Creek. In that city my father labored during the dark days of slavery to earn money to purchase my mother and two children. The memory of by-gone days came with powerful force over my mind, from what I had heard my parents speak of the place and people. There are many signs, as well as the elements, in that city, to make our people a great blessing to themselves and the world. Progress is the watch word and order of the day among them.